Thirty
DAYS UNTIL
I Die

AND ARGUING WITH MYSELF ABOUT IT

PT BATEMAN

THIRTY DAYS UNTIL I DIE

And Arguing With Myself About It

Written by:

PT Bateman

THIRTY DAYS UNTIL I DIE

And Arguing With Myself About It

Disclaimer

This is a work of fiction. Any names or characters, businesses or places, events, or incidents, are fictitious. Any resemblance to actual persons, living or dead, or actual events is purely coincidental.

Published by: PT Bateman

Cover Design: Kristina Conatser | Captured by KC Designs

ISBN: 979-8-218-08616-9

<u>*Dedication*</u>

Thank you, Tia.

Without you, Caroline wouldn't be the same

PROLOGUE

I sat across from the doctor and his masculine, mahogany desk. The room was painted in a false cheeriness of yellow that all doctors' offices seem to be painted. My hands gripped the arms of the leather chair. I waited with bated breath for him to speak. I knew what he was about to say but hoped he wouldn't say it just the same. I looked at his desk. Anything for a distraction. It was neat and orderly without a speck of dust to be found. Pens were placed in a silver cup that looked like it was given to him by some pharmaceutical company as a perk. He had a desk calendar in front of him with lots of writing I couldn't make out.

Like anyone could read a doctor's handwriting.

Behind him were a bunch of medical books stacked on a mahogany bookshelf, matching his desk, that he probably read for his residency but hadn't cracked open since then. The window behind him had bland, blue curtains pushed to the side, but the blinds were partially closed so they wouldn't shine too much light on the patient. The smell in the air was that of antiseptic-hospital antiseptic- so I knew I was in a place riddled with the lingering memories of sickness.

"Edna," He started softly. "There's no way to say this other than to the point. You have a very aggressive cancer. It's called metastatic lung cancer. I'm sure you've seen the commercials for its treatments. It's why you've been so tired lately and having trouble swallowing. Looking at your test results, the prognosis isn't very good. Unfortunately, we didn't catch it early enough." Dr. Linder finally said with his stoic, straight, doctor face.

"How long?" I asked coming back into focus.

"Given the aggressiveness of this type of cancer... I'm sorry to say, a month, maybe two."

The words hit me like a ton of bricks. The doctor was still talking. His lips were moving, and words were coming out of his mouth. "We can start chemotherapy to extend your time maybe another month or two. Modern medicine is making breakthroughs with new treatments, and I can try to get you into an experimental treatment option. I would suggest consulting with family members for the best course of action for you. I have a pamphlet with information about hospice care, and Kathleen, my oncology nurse, will set up an appointment for them to come out to your house if you'd like. I'm sorry. I know this isn't what you wanted to hear today. Do you want us to call a relative for you to pick you up? I thought I recommended that you bring along a family member. Are you here by yourself?" He asked with perceived sympathy.

I wasn't listening. His words were fading into the background, but my thoughts were becoming loud and clear.

What did he just say? A month? A month! What the hell am I going to do in a month?

I felt as if I wasn't even in the room. It was like I was watching some sappy soap opera where the unseasoned actor who played the doctor's role was sitting there, and I was the naïve patient looking at him with my mouth open.

Maybe I would get a Tony for the role. I can hear the audience cheering me on now. "Bravo! Bravo!" Well, that was a dumb thought. I'm not an actor. This isn't a soap opera. This is my LIFE! Well, the end of it apparently.

Cancer. That simple, six-letter, two-syllable word just hung in the air. Cancer. I guess that word didn't hit me as hard as 'month' did. *One month.* I couldn't even think about the "maybe two." *One month.* The words just stuck in my throat. *Thirty days. That's better, right? Thirty is more than one. Thirty days until I die.*

I must have stood up because the doctor was now standing. I walked over to him and shook his hand. I think I thanked him.

Why did I thank him? He just told me I was going to die, and I thanked him?

I guess we're just hardwired to be polite. I started to walk out of the office when the doctor called me back.

"Here's the information pamphlet for the local hospice center, and, as I said, Kathleen will set things up for you if you'd like." He said flatly.

Gee, thanks. Didn't want to forget that piece of information! I thanked him again and left the office.

As I walked towards the parking garage, my mind returned to that stupid, cheesy, soap opera scene. I pictured myself in that hospital bed staring blankly at the novice actor-doctor. My hand covered my mouth and tears began to fall. Although this wasn't a scene in my imagination playing out, this was real. I had to stop and catch myself. Tears were steadily streaming from my eyes. Snot was making its way out of my nose. To the passerby, I imagined I looked as if I just euthanized my favorite dog.

I can't do this. I was still sobbing. *Well, you don't really have a choice now, do you?* Sometimes, I just want to punch myself and tell myself to shut up!

Where's my car? I know I parked on Level 2. I grabbed my phone and opened the picture app. I always take a picture of where I park for this very reason. *Yep, Level 2. Now, where's my car?* I looked down the row where I thought I had parked my car, but I didn't see it. I walked over to the next row. Each row looked the same. The same red cars. The same white cars. I couldn't find my car in the sea of cars.

Where is my car? Where the hell is my car!? It's a black Mercedes, for Christ's sake. How many of them are in this garage? I worked hard for this car and now I was going to have to give it away. Some other person was going to drive my hard-earned car because I was going to die. *Hey stupid, get your keys out and hit the unlock button. Shut up!* Well, wouldn't you know? It worked. I found my car and got in.

I couldn't move as I sat behind the steering wheel. I just sat there, frozen in place. *Lung cancer. Oh, no, not just any old lung cancer. Metastatic lung cancer. Let's not forget the big "m" word to go along with it.* I flung myself back in the seat. I felt myself getting angry. I wanted to punch something. I wanted to punch something so hard that whatever it was I punched would feel as bad as I did.

"Here, hit Ouisa!" *Holy shit! What is it with me? Now, I'm reciting movie quotes.* And I can't get the damn scene out of my head.

"I want to hit something. I want to hit it hard." Yep, *Steel Magnolias* was running through my mind.

Okay, get a grip. You need to leave and get yourself home and get stuff in order. Stuff? What kind of stuff? I don't know. Stuff. Everyone must get stuff in order when they are getting ready to die. What about people who get hit by a bus? Did they get stuff in order? Well, no, but this isn't the same thing. You have thirty days to get stuff in order. You've been given a chance. Oh, yeah, a chance. Thanks. Shut up!

I started to back out of my parking space when I noticed a car waiting for my spot. *Not now, buddy. Don't you even think about rushing me out of my parking space! I'm dying. You're living. I'm taking my sweet time.* And I did. I must have spent at least three long, agonizing minutes carefully getting out of the parking space. Backing up, pulling forward, acting like I was scared to scratch the cars next to me. I finally cleared the spot, and he immediately dashed into it with his horn blaring, a few choice words, and a beautifully manicured middle finger to send me on my way. I chuckled to myself.

You can be such a bitch sometimes. Don't I know it!

DAY ONE

Shit! I'm still alive. Why couldn't I have just died while I was sleeping? It would have been so much easier, right? I mean, I wouldn't have to start making plans. I wouldn't have to tell my children. I wouldn't have to tell my mom. Oh, crap. How is mom going to take this? Children are supposed to outlive their parents. At least, that's what everyone says, and everyone must be right. Why can't they just be wrong? Why can't the doctor just be wrong? Why can't this whole thing just be wrong?

I rolled over and got myself out of bed. I walked down the hallway and made my usual morning stop at the bathroom. As I looked in the mirror, I thought, *I don't look sick. I don't look like I'm dying. I look the same as I did yesterday. Eh, the hair is a mess, but have you seen how you sleep?*

Look. I got a new pimple. Fifty-eight years old, and I'm still getting pimples. Seriously? I looked closely. I looked to see if it was ready to pop. I could just pop it onto the mirror if it had that little white build-up. It wasn't ready. *Maybe tomorrow. You should still be around for the final popping.*

I finished up in the bathroom and headed into the kitchen. I got the coffee started and sat down at the table placing my head in my hands. *Thirty days.* I looked at the calendar hanging on by magnets on the refrigerator. *Today is July 2.* I got up and rumbled through the junk drawer that every single person in America has in their kitchen and found a red Sharpie pen. I circled the day... *July 30. Yep, that's the one.* Printed so innocently on the calendar.

That's the day I'm going to die. Stop it! You don't know that for sure. The doctor said "maybe two" months. Okay, fine. I'll circle August 30, too. Does that make you feel better? Not really.

I opened the refrigerator to get my hazelnut coffee creamer. I looked at the contents of the refrigerator holding the creamer in my hand. There were several containers of leftovers from the past few days' dinners. I hated leftovers. I don't know why I kept them. They would just stay in the refrigerator until mold set in, and I would throw them out. Sitting in one container was spaghetti noodles and meat sauce from Tuesday night. A container of a leftover roast from Wednesday was shoved in the back of the second shelf, complete with potatoes and chopped onions. In another container laid steamed shrimp I swore I'd make shrimp salad out of. That one was starting to become a petri dish of penicillin.

Wow, that's a lot of food! It's enough to last more than a month. Well, maybe not. You're probably going to start losing weight quickly and maybe you'll eat it all. Except for the shrimp. Throw that out. Again, with the negative thoughts? Yes, face it. You're going to lose weight. A lot of it! Well, maybe I'll just start eating whatever I want and throw out all this good-for-you food away. I'll go to the store and buy everything in the bakery department and eat cake, cookies, and doughnuts for the time I have left. How's that for a plan? I'm okay with that. You never eat doughnuts anyway, so this should be fun! Fun? I'm dying. This isn't fun.

I poured too much creamer into the coffee and decided to use real sugar instead of my usual stevia packet. *Why not? Don't want to leave sugar around after I'm gone. The kids might not get to it before the ants do.* The ants always seem to find their way in during the summer months, especially after the heavy rains. It's like they are looking for a dry place to hang out.

The coffee was overly sweet, but I didn't care. It wasn't as hot as it usually was probably because of the extra creamer. I sat there sipping my coffee. Just me and my thoughts.

What did I miss? Why didn't they catch it in time?

You know why. You hate going to the doctor's office. You don't like the receptionist because she's too matter of fact. Every time you try to make small talk, she brushes you off by handing you paperwork to fill out. You haven't been to see a doctor in over two years. You should have gone when you first started having trouble swallowing.

I had been to my regular Monday night trivia. God, how I loved playing trivia. Our team was awesome, winning every four out of five games. We were only a team of three, but each of us had our strengths, some of them overlapping. Kim was excellent with television and movie trivia. Robbie was the best at anything presidential or geographical. I had a knack for literature and history. All three of us had the ability to pick out music artists as that was a component of the game. Together we had a great time answering questions and talking about our lives during the week.

I ordered some fries and a beer. The bar made great steak fries. They are always crispy, and golden brown with a soft middle and just enough salt added. As I started to eat my fries, it felt like one got caught in my throat.

No problem, I'll just wash it down with a cold beer.

That seemed to have gotten stuck too. I coughed a little to try and jar the contents down. The beer and fries started to go down, but it was slow and difficult. After that, I took smaller bites. Swallowing still felt uncomfortable, but I didn't think much of it and enjoyed the rest of the night.

About a month later, it happened again. This time I was home alone. I had just made my favorite dinner; a medium-well done New York strip steak, baked potato, and corn on the cob. A nice cold beer, to enhance the food, sat to the right of my plate. It all looked and smelled so good. The melted butter and chives sat tantalizingly on top of the split of the baked potato. The steak I had drizzled with sautéed mushrooms and the corn on the cob dripped with butter, salt, and pepper. I sat down to eat, cut a piece of steak, and dipped it in some A-1 sauce. It got stuck. I started to gag and cough.

Put your hands over your head.

I put my hands over my head, still coughing. Tears streaming down my red face like that makes a difference when you're coughing your head off! Finally, after what seemed like an eternity, it went down.

As time went by, I just started cutting up my food into smaller and smaller pieces and drinking some sort of liquid, mainly soda or beer, between bites to help wash it down. That seemed to help for a while. Until it didn't. I also noticed that I was unusually tired more often. I mean, I was no spring chicken, but by six o'clock at night, I felt like I had been run over by a truck. That's when I went to the doctor's office. That's when I filled out the paperwork given to me by the coldhearted, unenthusiastic receptionist. That's when I had blood work done. That was the beginning of the end.

I want a cigarette.

You quit smoking two years ago. You probably should have quit long before that. You might not be where you are now. Don't you think that thought hasn't crossed my mind? I mean, you're here, too! Oh, but a cigarette would be so nice right now. Taking a long drag, watch the tobacco burn down on the filter, hold the smoke in my mouth for a second or two, and then let out a long puff of white smoke watching as it blows away in the air.

Yeah, I want a cigarette.

I sat at the table a little while longer before I decided to watch the morning news. When the weatherman revealed the forecast for the week, I just lost it. He was giving the forecast as if what he was saying was the most important information anyone would need to help them plan out their wardrobe for the next seven days.

Suddenly, my eyes started watering, and I just could not stop them. People watching him tuned in without a care in the world. They looked at each day with a plan in their mind as to how the rest of their week was going to be. They needed to know whether to take an umbrella or not. They weren't thinking about their limited time on Earth. The unfairness of it all sank into my soul. I wasn't even thinking. I was just crying. Crying hard. The sobs racked my body so much that I started having trouble breathing.

Is this what it's going to feel like? Gasping for breath in my last and final moments.

I suddenly thought of all those crime shows where the victim is found with a plastic bag over their head.

Maybe I should do that now. Get it over with. Sure, leave it to someone else to find you with a bag over your head. Then the police will be called and an investigation into the supposed crime. Hey, maybe I'd make the local headline news. 'Local woman found with a Harry's Grocery Market bag taped around her head. No suspects in the matter for now. An autopsy will be performed to determine the cause of death.'

What would Kevin and Amelia think? Man, that would surely cause some reaction. Kevin and Amelia. My two precious children. Well, they're not really children anymore. Both are grown with children of their own.

I had two grandchildren too, ages two and six. One from each of my children. So precious those babies were when they were born. I closed my eyes and could still smell that scent all newborns have. It was a mixture of love, baby lotion, and baby body wash. *Those companies really know how to work your senses. Kind of like that new car smell. It instantly transports you to a specific memory.*

"It will be a typical July week for our area," he said. "Highs will be in the upper 80s and overnight temperatures will be muggy and in the 70s. We may have some cooler weather coming into the area thanks to a passing cold front starting early next week." I stared at the weatherman's suit. He was nicely dressed in a solid, dark grey suit. His tie didn't seem to pair with the suit, though. It was neon pink and had bold, bright purple triangles on it.

What was he thinking when he got dressed this morning? I wonder what the temperature will be on the day I die. Stop it. I don't want to stop it. I need to have it all planned out. I need to think about every single aspect of it. I'm dying. Don't you get it? Yes, I get it. More than you know.

Suddenly, I let out a blood-curdling scream. I mean, I just opened my mouth and screamed. I wasn't even sure what I was screaming about. Pain? Fear? Guilt? The utter unfairness of it all?

My neighbor, Delores, who lived two doors over must have heard me scream because she started knocking frantically on my front door. I opened the door, and my face must have shocked her. Delores had moved into the neighborhood about twelve years ago after she found out her husband of fifteen years had been cheating on her with his secretary. She was a medium-sized woman in her late fifties, like me, with the wildest red hair you've ever seen. She could have been a flower child if she had just been born a decade earlier. I hadn't liked her at first because she was a nosey neighbor that was always coming around when I was outside to ask if she could help with anything. She acted as if she was the know-it-all of gardening, weeding, and power-washing, giving me tidbits of information on the precise way to do each.

Eventually, she grew on me when I realized that she was just lonely and looking for a friend. Her seemingly obnoxious manner was all a ruse as she had just been trying to make conversation. We became fast friends and would go to dinners, movies, concerts, and whatever else two single women wanted to get into without the hassle of men always trying to ask us out.

"Are you okay?" She asked. "I was watching the morning news, and I heard this scream coming from your direction."

"I'm fine, Delores." I lied. "I thought I saw a snake under the refrigerator." I lied again. She must not have fallen for my little lie. Maybe she saw an invisible post-it note stuck to my forehead that said, *"30 days and counting."*

"You don't look so good," she said with concern in her eyes.

"I'm just a little under the weather, Delores. Thanks for checking on me," I said, trying to gently push her back out the door.

"Okay. If you need anything, just give me a holler. Just not so scary next time, okay?" she said as she exited.

I smiled and waved bye. Delores left, and I shut the front door.

That went over well, don't you think? Well, I'm not ready to tell anyone yet. Not even the kids? Not even mom, your friends, the rest of the family? No, no one. I need to just sit here and let it sink in.

DAY TWO

What time is it? Time to get your butt out of bed. I rolled over and looked at the clock. 10:30. *What? 10:30? I never sleep this late. You did today. I'm tired. I'm just tired, that's all. No, you're tired because you're dying. Would you just stop? Nope, not going to do it. I need to call mom and the kids. What are you going to say? I don't know yet.*

I got out of bed and did the bathroom thing. The pimple was still there but getting smaller. *That's good, the funeral home won't have to use too much makeup then. Does the undertaker pop un-popped zits?*

I went into the kitchen, started the coffee going, and looked around for something to eat. I wasn't very hungry. *Told you that you'd start to lose weight. Shut up, okay?* For that thought, I promptly made a scrambled egg sandwich. I even loaded it with butter! I added salt and pepper to taste. It was delicious!

After breakfast, I went into the living room to get my phone. I never liked having the phone right next to me at night. If it was that important to call me in the middle of the night, leave a message, or better yet, come over and tell me. I'd handle it in the morning. I picked up the phone and just stared at it in my hands.

Whom are you going to call first, the kids or mom? I better call mom. It's probably going to be the toughest one to handle. Are you going to tell her over the phone? Yes. Really? No. I'll invite her over for lunch today. What are you going to fix for lunch? Would you just let me call first and stop asking so many questions? Suit yourself, I'm just thinking about lunch.

"Hey, Mom. How are you doing?" I asked, trying to sound upbeat.

"I'm hot," she stated. Mom never did like the heat. She didn't like the cold either. I think it was the humidity that made her not like the heat. And it does get mighty humid in Louisiana in July!

"Are you busy today? I wanted to talk to you about what the doctor said at my appointment." I said, still trying to sound upbeat.

She didn't bite. "What's wrong? What did he say? Why don't you just tell me?" She fired off the questions.

"Mom, come over for lunch today and we'll talk," I said, sounding deflated.

She started crying. "Lunch? You can't tell me over the phone. Oh, God. It must be bad news. It is bad news, isn't it?" She was starting to get hysterical. Her voice was starting to climb.

"Mom, just come over. I don't want to explain all of it over the phone." I kept my emotions in check.

She didn't say anything. I think she was waiting for me to relent and just spill the beans. *Two can play this game, Mom.* I didn't say another word. "Okay. I'll be there around noon." She finally said, giving up the fight. We said our goodbyes and hung up.

Mom was right. It was hot. And humid. If she was going to be here by noon, I had better get myself dressed. I put on a pair of shorts and a tank top and made my way to the kitchen again.

What am I going to fix for lunch? I asked you that already. Why don't you fix something cold to eat? It's hot outside. Well, thank you Captain Obvious!

I gathered stuff together to make a nice salad. I made two individual bowls since mom didn't like grapes in her salad and I did. I looked in the cabinet and got some canned chicken out, drained it, and then seasoned it. I topped the salad with the chicken and placed the bowls on the table with a couple of different dressings to choose from. Blue cheese dressing for me and a choice of Ranch, Balsamic Vinaigrette, or Thousand Island for mom.

Suddenly, I started coughing again. The cough lasted for what seemed like twenty minutes, but it was only less than a minute. I reached over the sink and got a paper towel to spit out what had gathered in my mouth. Blood. *Well, that's not a good sign. Nope. You need to find that Hospice pamphlet Dr. Linder gave you and call them soon. I know, but I need to talk to mom and the kids today. It can wait until tomorrow. If you say so.*

The doorbell rang. I quickly threw the paper towel away. *Better bury that paper towel in the trash so your mom doesn't see it.* Mom didn't wait for me to answer the door; she bolted through it.

"Edna" was all she said. Mom folded her arms around me and gave me a powerful bear hug. She was quite strong for a 92-year-old woman. I even tried to take her driver's license away a few years back, but she went to a driver's education refresher course and passed with flying colors. There was no arguing with her about it after that. When she pulled back, tears were streaming down her face.

"What did the doctor say?" she asked, concerned.

"Come into the kitchen and sit down, Mom," I said as I guided her into the kitchen. We sat down and I took her hands into mine. Tears welled up in my eyes as I stared into hers. I cleared my throat. "I have cancer, Mom. It's not good. It's not good at all. There is no easy way to say this, Mom. The doctor told me I have about a month, maybe two to live. It is progressing rapidly, and there is nothing they can do except keep me comfortable until it's time."

As the words came out of my mouth, I watched my mom's face slowly droop. The news was draining her. She stared at me with tears silently rolling down her cheeks. The color faded from her cheeks. Her wrinkled hands started to shake in mine.

"Oh, Edna." She sobbed. "What can I do? How can I help? How is this possible? You're too young." She rapidly fired off the questions.

"It's my fault, mom. I should have taken better care of myself." I replied. "I'm going to call the funeral home later today and set up an appointment to make funeral arrangements, and then I'm going to call hospice to get someone in here to help out."

"Have you told Kevin or Amelia?" She asked. "Not yet," I replied. "I will. I'm going to see if they both can come over for dinner tonight, so I don't have to say it to one before the other. Neither one would take too kindly to one knowing before the other, and I don't want the accusation of whom I loved better."

Mom sat there staring off into space, not saying a word. *Now you've done it. You need to cheer her up before she has a heart attack. And just how do you propose I do that? "Hey mom, sorry I dropped a death bomb on ya, but how about we go to the comedy club tomorrow night and just laugh about it all?" Yeah, and how do you think she'll reply to that? I have no idea.*

Mom and I sat there for the longest time in silence. She aimlessly ate her salad, one bite at a time. I wasn't too hungry since I ate the scrambled eggs only an hour or so before.

"You're not eating." She noticed.

"I just ate a little before you got here, mom, so I'm not very hungry." *Liar! You scarfed down that egg sandwich quickly enough. That was to spite you!*

"You should eat." She responded.

Ha! Told you! Well, I said you were going to lose weight. I never said how. Sure, you stick with that excuse for losing an argument. I haven't lost yet.

Mom and I finished our lunch and put the dishes in the sink. I could tell she was at a loss for words about what to say or do next.

"I'm going to be okay, Mom. I've had an entire day to think about all the things I need and want to do. Am I devastated at the news? Of course, I am. Do I want to change this? Of course, I do. I can't. Right now, I'm only having some trouble breathing and I get tired quickly. I imagine that will get worse. I don't want anyone to be sad. I can't bear seeing people cry every time they see me. I'm even going to have a party later this month."

"A party?" She asked. "I don't think that's such a good idea, Edna." She said scornfully. "You should rest as much as possible. You could exacerbate the situation by overdoing yourself."

"Yes, Mom, a party." I huffed. "I don't want my last days filled with sorrow and remorse. I don't want people to remember me that way. I want a party with live music, lots of food, lots of drinks, and lots of fun." *I thought you didn't want fun. Shut up.* "It will also give people a chance to say goodbye while I'm still here on this Earth. You know how I never wanted a big to-do when it came to my funeral. Just stick me in a pine box and put me in the ground."

She started crying again from that mental picture. "Please, Mom, don't cry. I need you to be strong for me. I need you to be strong for the kids when I'm gone."

"Who's going to be strong for me?" She softly asked.

"I don't know, Mom. I just don't know." I said deflated.

Mom left and I sat down on the couch for a bit. I must have dozed off. I woke up and looked at the clock. The time was 4:07. *Wow! It's that late already? I need to call the kids. Too late to start fixing something for dinner. No? Really? I couldn't figure that out myself. You're such a smart ass sometimes. What is your point? Dinner is off the table, so to speak. How about dessert? Desert and dying. What a combination. It gives a whole different meaning to death by chocolate.*

I picked up the phone and dialed Kevin. He is the oldest of my two children. At thirty, Kevin had finally grown up. His teenage years were a little rough sometimes. His father and I had divorced when he was ten. He didn't take it very well. Kevin started hanging around the wrong type of friends and would get in trouble at school because of it. The kids he was hanging around weren't violent, just mischievous, but still detrimental to Kevin's attitude and grades. Many times, the school would call saying Kevin was acting up in class, flipping some kid's books out of his hands, or smoking in the bathrooms. Either his father or I would have to go down to the school, pick him up, and dole out some sort of punishment.

It took about two years of this before Kevin straightened up and got rid of those so-called friends. Kevin finished high school and did well enough to get a scholarship to the state university. He probably partied a little too much at first, but when he met Paula that all changed.

They dated throughout the remainder of his college years. Kevin was head over heels for Paula. She kept him focused on school and the future. When they graduated, he proposed. Kevin and Paula settled down and started a family. Gracie was born two years after they got married.

My ex-husband Russell, was, and still is, a good dad. He went to all of Kevin's soccer games, kept up with making sure his grades were good, and took him and his sister on vacation every summer. Russell had the kids every other weekend and called them at least three times a week to check in on them. We stayed friends throughout the kids' growing up years; we just weren't good as a romantic couple.

You need to call Russell too. I know.

"Hey, Kev, how are things with you?" I started the conversation.

"Mom! What good timing you have. Paula and Gracie just left for the park." It was hard to talk sometimes with Kevin when Gracie was around. She was a very, very active six-year-old that doesn't understand the concept of phone conversations that don't involve her. There had been many times Kevin had to call me back once Gracie was asleep just so we could hold a normal conversation without her interruptions.

"Oh, that's nice. Hey, can you come over around 8 o'clock tonight?" I asked.

"Sure, what's up?" He inquired; concern tainted his voice.

"I want to talk to you and your sister about what the doctor said." Again, I was trying to sound upbeat, but Kevin wasn't falling for it either.

"From your tone, Mom, this doesn't sound like good news." He stated, very concerned.

"To be honest, Kevin, it isn't good news. That's why I want to talk to you and Amelia tonight." I was just too tired to try and keep the conversation light. I wanted to get all this talking about it, letting everyone know, and re-hashing the same news over and over done with. It was like a record that was stuck in the same groove. And this was only the second person I had spoken to. I had many more conversations to get through.

"Okay, mom. Paula and I will be there at 8 o'clock." He said after I didn't finish my line of speaking. "I'll ask Paula to see if Candice can stay here with Gracie. I think she's home from college and would love to babysit Gracie." Kevin had nervousness in his voice, but he knew better than to push for more information over the phone, knowing I wouldn't provide it.

"Thanks, son. I agree that Gracie should stay home; it's not a conversation that she needs to hear right now. I won't keep you long." I promised.

I hung up with Kevin and called Amelia.

Amelia had been a free spirit ever since she was a little girl. She had the bubbliest personality and could light up a room with her smile. I remembered when Russell and I threw Amelia's fifth birthday party. We invited the entire block of kids. We had the bouncy castle, slip and slide, and a little photo booth filled with princess and cowboy props. Russell even rented a pony for the day. Amelia rode that pony all day long, waving her wand around all the kids turning them into imaginary frogs, puppies, and alligators. She only let the other kids ride the pony when she decided she wanted something to eat.

Amelia traveled after she graduated from high school. She didn't know what she wanted to do as far as a career was concerned so she thought by traveling she'd figure something out. She met Tony in Brazil, fell in love, and got married. Tony was a very handsome man and had the charm all South Americans seem to have. He loved Amelia, or so he thought. He was too much of a romantic to be tied down to one woman. Amelia suffered the consequences of it.

After about a month, she realized Tony was a mistake and filed for divorce. When she came home, she realized that during that one month of marriage, she had gotten pregnant with Henry. Tony didn't know about Henry, and I doubt he ever will. He wouldn't be responsible enough to support Henry anyway. Amelia's love for Henry settled her down some and now she works as an office manager for a well-to-do law firm and has started taking paralegal classes.

"Hi, Mom!"

How did she know it was me? I kept forgetting that whole caller ID thing that they have on phones. "Hi, sweetie. How are you today?" Again, I was trying to sound upbeat.

"Mom, you won't believe it. Henry threw his ball all the way across the backyard!" Henry just turned two in April. She was too excited about the news she was telling me to notice the fake, bubbly tone of my voice.

"That's great! He's going to be the next Randy Johnson!" I exclaimed.

"Who's that?" she asked.

Don't kids know anything?

"He was a famous pitcher for the Seattle Mariners. Really tall guy," I huffed.

"Oh. I don't think Henry is going to be very tall. Tony was only 5 feet 7 inches tall." She said densely, as I faced palmed myself.

"Hey, sweetie," I said getting back to the conversation at hand. "I was wondering if you could get a sitter for Henry for about an hour tonight and come over around 8 o'clock. Kevin is coming over too. There's something I need to discuss with you two, and I don't want any distractions. Not that Henry is a distraction, I just want your undivided attention."

"Sure, Mom. Is everything all right?" she said with concern.

"Not really. I went to see Dr. Linder the other day, and I want to talk to you two about what he said."

"Mom? Are you okay?"

Can somebody please find another way to ask that question? Maybe, "the presentation of your conversation has led me to assume that things are not as stable as they should be. Am I correct in my assumption?" Who talks like that? Well, Shakespeare maybe. This is the twenty-first century, no one talks like that!

"Honey, no. But I don't want to talk over the phone about it," I sighed with a tone that said to Amelia to stop inquiring.

"Okay, Mom. Stephanie has been asking if she could watch Henry for weeks now. I'll give her a call and see if she could watch him tonight." Her voice sounded worried, as she realized that the news, I was going to tell her wasn't going to be good.

"Thank you. I won't keep you long. I know Stephanie can be a little expensive." I stated.

I should probably eat before the kids get here. There's an entire refrigerator full of food that you need to eat before you go. Go? I'm not going on vacation, you know. I'm not going to the store. I'm not going for a bike ride. I'm the "big one" going.

"It's the big one, Elizabeth." Fred Sanford echoed in my head.

Either way, you need to eat something. Who delivers? I want something delivered. And leave the food in the refrigerator? Yep. I don't feel like fixing anything. Order a pizza.

The local pizza place delivered my dinner within thirty minutes. I sat down and ate one slice of pizza. *That's it? Yep. I'm not hungry.*

I heard Kevin's and Amelia's cars pull up into the driveway at the same time. I greeted them at the door with a plastered smile on my face. We gave each other customary hugs and sat down in the living room.

"Where's Paula?" I asked Kevin.

"She and I thought it would be best if she stayed home. Gracie had been getting a little sleepy, and you know how cranky she can get when she's tired. No sense and putting that on Candice to deal with. She said that I could let her know what was going on when I get home." Kevin was trying not to say that Paula had a bad feeling and thought it would be better if it were just him and Amelia talking with me.

"There's no easy way to say this, so I'm just going to say it. Dr. Linder said that I have lung cancer. It's metastatic and the most aggressive. He has given me a month, maybe two to live." There was just dead silence as the words hung in the air. I could tell by the look on Kevin and Amelia's faces that the words were slowly sinking in.

"A month? You have to be kidding me!" Kevin started the conversation. "They can't find a way to fix it? There's nothing they can do; no experimental treatment they can start? I mean, I just saw a commercial for something called proton therapy where they zap the tumor or whatever and you're cured. How are you going to pay for the care?"

Visions of me and the kids running around a laser tag arena with them shooting their laser guns at my chest trying to zap the cancer away enter my mind.

"No, honey," I said. "They can't treat this. It's too far along; there's nothing they can do." I was deflated. "As far as the hospice care costs and all that goes with it, my insurance is going to cover all of it. You won't have to worry about any hospital bills."

"Why didn't you tell us when all this started, Mom?" Kevin was getting angry. "You knew that something major was wrong, and you didn't think to tell us? We could have gone with you. We could have spoken to the doctor with you. But you decide to lay all this on us after the fact? What the hell, Mom?"

"Kevin, calm down," I said, anger rising in me now. *You know, telling a person to calm down only infuriates the person. No shit, Sherlock. But he's pissing me off now. I'm a grown woman, I can make choices on my own. I can speak to the doctor by myself if I want to.*

Amelia had been very quiet. "What are you going to do, mom?" She asked.

I'm going to die, that's what I'm going to do. Stop it! You know she has such a big heart and can't stand to see people suffer or be in pain. I know. I'll stop. It's just so hard being strong sometimes.

"I'm going to do the best that I can do with what I'm given, sweetie," I said softly. I needed to refocus and calm myself. Nothing good would come out of a shouting match with Kevin, and it obviously wouldn't help Amelia either.

"I know this is hard to hear and I know you have so many thoughts and questions going through your head. It is what it is. Do I like it? No. I really don't. I'm calling the funeral home tomorrow and setting up an appointment to meet with the funeral director. I need to figure out what type of ceremony to have for everyone. You know if it were up to me, I wouldn't have any funeral at all. But I know you guys need that closure," I said, deflated.

I looked over at Amelia and Kevin. I had been staring off into space as I spoke the words. I couldn't bear to see their faces right now, and I had to get out what I needed to say. As I suspected, both had tears streaming down their faces. It hurt so much to see my children suffering. Kevin's anger was simply deep-rooted sorrow. I wanted to hold them and tell them that everything was going to be okay. I'm the mommy. I'm supposed to make everything better. This time, there wasn't a damn thing I could do to comfort my children. I wanted to scream at God at the total unfairness.

Hey, you did this. You brought this on. You can make it go away. How about throwing me one of those miracles, huh?

God wasn't listening.

I gathered some maternal strength to ease their pain. "I don't want either of you to feel pressured to speak at my funeral. If you want to, go ahead. If you don't, I won't hold it against you."

What are you going to do? Haunt them?

"I'll let you know what I decide once I have my meeting with the funeral director. There's no need for you two to go. I know it would be hard on you, so I'm just going to make the arrangements myself. You both know basically what I want, no fanfare with multiple viewing services. One viewing, one service, and there will be an interment, but that's just going to be us. In the meantime, I'm going to have a going away party, so to speak."

"A going away party?" Kevin asked, confused.

"Yep. While I have some strength left, I want a party," I said sitting straight up, puffing out my chest. "I want to be surrounded by my friends and family with some good music and some good food and just a fun, well maybe not fun, but a good time. If that makes any sense."

Let's have live music. Call up some band and say, 'Hey, wanna play at my funeral party?' Sure, why don't we call Make-A-Wish and get some famous band like Led Zeppelin or Aerosmith or Rush? Rush doesn't play together anymore. Yeah, right. Maybe they'll play in Heaven when they all get there.

"I think that's a great idea, Mom." Amelia finally said. She still sounded choked up but cleared her throat and continued. "I can get a few days off from work and help you get things together. I can go over to the party store and get plates, cutlery, and that kind of stuff if you want." I could tell she was trying to keep it together and party planning was just the ticket to distract her.

"That would be wonderful, sweetie," I replied. "I have phone calls to make tomorrow to let people know I'm throwing an impromptu party. Do you think I should let them know why? I don't want them to think it's something that they could miss, but I also don't want them to miss it when they realize that it's the last party. You know what I mean."

"Tell them the why, Mom," Kevin said. "I'm not sure what all information you can tell them. I mean, do you say, 'Hey, come to my series finale?"

"Kevin, that's a perfect idea! I want to keep it light but also want them to be able to say their goodbyes if they want to."

How much liquor are you going to have? Really? Do you want people to get drunk? No, I want to! Okay, I can agree with that.

"I can take care of calling everyone, Mom." Amelia volunteered.

"Oh, that would be great. I'll give you a list of people I'd like to invite and their phone numbers before you leave." I was relieved Amelia took the burden off my shoulders.

The kids and I chatted a little more about this and that. We got out of that deep, dark conversation enough to end the night on a lighter note. I just couldn't bear to stay in that space for very long. I knew this was a serious situation, but I had to keep things light, or I wouldn't be able to do anything but lay in bed and drool until the end.

"I love you, Mom," Kevin and Amelia said at the same time.

"I love you both so much," I said as they turned to leave. I handed Amelia the list. I closed the door before they could see the tears rolling down my face again. I slowly slid down the inside of the door, knees bending as my butt hit the floor. I just sat on the floor, in front of the door, staring off into nothing, unable to move.

DAY THREE

"Edna? Edna, are you there?" Delores was knocking very loudly on my front door. What time is it? 11:30 AM. Jesus, I slept in! You'll sleep when you're dead; now get up!

"Hang on, Delores," I yelled so she could hear me. I opened the door and in flew Delores. *Don't look at her mole.* I looked. I couldn't help myself.

"Oh, Edna!" Delores said, grabbing me in a little too snug bear hug. "I'm so sorry."

"Sorry, for what?" I said still staring at the mole just sitting there on her chin waiting to be commented on.

"Amelia called me last night." *Of course, she did. Don't you just love it? Stop! She means well and she just doesn't know what to do. I know, I know. "Is there anything I can do?" Yeah, take this cancer away. Do you have a laser tag gun?*

"Delores. How long have we known each other? Ten... Twelve years?" I asked. "We've been through some crazy times together and right now; I need you to be my crazy neighbor. I need to keep focused but I also don't want to be depressed for the last few weeks of my life. Can you be that kind of friend to me?"

"Anything, Edna. Anything." She said. "I will only talk about the happy, wild times we've had. But do allow me to say how much I will miss you. I will miss our time together. I mean who else could I have butt-mooned Harold with when we saw him and Caroline eating dinner over at Charlie's Grill? Remember the look on their faces when we walked by that restaurant where they were eating, caught their attention, turned around, and just pulled down our pants?" She and I started laughing about that.

She had a thong on, she didn't have to pull down anything. That was funny, too!!

Delores really did not like Caroline. Caroline was too sophisticated and snotty. I guess Harold had trouble dealing with Delores' free-spirited style and carefree manner and wanted someone with a pole up their ass. He found that in Caroline.

Delores reminded me of me, and I think that's why we got along so well. I was a carefree person in my younger days. I was educated, somewhat good-looking, and had a sharp wit about me that sometimes took people by surprise. I would drink my friends under the table and never wake up with a hangover. I probably was born a decade too late. I would have made a great teenage flower child, but the sixties were over before I reached that age.

I never thought about the downside of adulthood until Russell and I had kids. Then I had to be the responsible one. I had to make the decisions for the family. I took over the bill paying because Russell just couldn't get a handle on it, and the collectors started calling. The process made me sarcastic and sometimes bitter. It wasn't fair that he could just turn everything over to me and maintain his "someone else would take care of it" attitude.

Yeah, that someone was me!

I eventually got in a better place mentally. I lost my grudge, for the most part, with Russell. I learned to focus on the simple things in life like reading and gardening. I found nature brought me peace and some semblance of sanity. I learned to take things in stride just as Delores had.

"There is something you can help me with, Delores. I need to go over to the funeral home and set up the arrangements. Is that asking too much?"

Immediately, Delores' reaction changed. "Of course not." She said solemnly. "When do you want to go?"

Um, no time like the present. "Let me change clothes and we can leave in about a half hour if that's okay? Why don't you grab some coffee while you wait?"

True to my word, Delores and I left the house within thirty minutes and headed over to Ford's Funeral Home. It was a ten-minute drive, and Delores didn't say one word on the way over.

"Ready?" She asked as we pulled into the parking lot.

"Do I have a choice?" I asked.

"Not really unless you want me to bury you in the backyard."

That's the spirit, Delores! Plant some daisies while you're at it. Get it? Pushing up daisies!

"Good afternoon, ladies. How may I help you?" We were greeted at the door by Mr. Thorn, Funeral Director. At least, that's what it said on his pristine name tag pinned on his pristine grey suit with his pristine haircut. I mean not one single peppered-grey hair seemed out of place.

"We need to speak to someone about funeral arrangements," Delores stated firmly.

"Of course, right this way. We can speak in my office," Mr. Thorn guided us to his pristine office.

"How may I help with your loved one's arrangements?" He asked with a kind and respectful tone.

"Do you perform Viking funerals? You know, the one where they put the body on a boat, send it down the river and then shoot a flaming arrow directly into the chest of the body and the whole thing goes up in flames?" Delores asked with the most serious expression on her face.

Mr. Thorn did not appreciate the humor and was staring intently at Delores' chin-mole. I snorted as I looked over at him.

"How about a Kriah? You know, tearing one's clothes. Is that allowed? She's Jewish." Mr. Thorn was not pleased and started to turn somewhat red in the face. He especially did not approve of me holding back my laughing at the whole exchange.

"I'm sorry, ladies, but you seem to find this very funny, and we here at Ford's Funeral Home take our business very seriously. I'm going to have to ask you to leave." Mr. Thorn started to stand up, brushing the fold out of his suit to maintain his pristine appearance.

"I'm sorry for my friend's indiscretion, Sir," I said, trying to diffuse the situation. "She's just following my orders to keep some humor in all this. I'm the one who needs arrangements. My name is Edna Berman. My doctor has told me that I will probably not live much longer. He's given me a month, maybe two. I want to get everything in order so that when my time comes, my children will not have to make these arrangements. The quickness of all this is already too much for them to bear."

Mr. Thorn sat back in his chair. His regular complexion starting to come back to his face. "I see. What arrangements are you looking for, other than a Viking funeral? Your friend stated you're Jewish, would you like to look into Jewish customs for your funeral?" He eyed Delores silently scolding her for the whole tearing-of-the-clothing comments.

"I'm only Jewish from my marriage to my, now, ex-husband, who never followed the faith. And, no, I don't want a Viking funeral, although the thought is intriguing. I want something simple. A pine box would be preferable, but I understand state laws won't allow such things. Do you rent caskets? I plan on being cremated and I don't want to waste money on something you're just going to throw into the incinerator."

"I think we can accommodate you, Ms. Berman. Why don't we look over some options?" Mr. Thorn pulled out some brochures, and we began making some decisions.

Delores and I finished making the arrangements with Mr. Thorn. I decided on a rented grey casket, that would not be incinerated, and some Bible verses to be read by my Pastor (after I realized I needed to call him as well).

I especially liked Psalm 62 verses 1-2: *"I wait quietly before God, for my victory comes from him. He alone is my rock and my salvation, my fortress where I will never be shaken."*

I'm not a fanatically religious person, but I do have my faith and right now, I needed God's fortress. Delores and I also picked out some music to be played during the memorial. Mr. Thorn did not think it was appropriate to include AD/DC's "Highway to Hell" during the ceremony. *Such a party pooper.* He did agree to allow "Spirit in the Sky" by Norman Greenbaum. *A compromise.*

After we left the funeral home, Delores asked if I wanted to get something to eat. I was a little hungry, so we decided to drive over to Pete's BBQ. It was a local staple that was always filled with customers licking their fingers while they ate their BBQ ribs. The place wasn't one of those high-end restaurants that you see showcased on TV, with the waitstaff in crisp white shirts and black pants asking if you had reservations or not. However, it sure had great food at a great price, and the people of the town just loved it.

"What do you think about having Pete's cater my party?" I asked Delores as we were driving.

"What party?" She inquired.

"Amelia didn't tell you about me wanting a going away party?"

"No, she didn't. But that is a great idea!" She said excitedly.

"Thanks. I thought so too. Can you help by letting people know about it? We have the same social media friends so you could just set up an event and invite people."

"That sounds like a good plan. We'll call it Edna's Ending Endeavor, or something along those lines," Delores joked.

That sounds like a great party theme! Delores is crazy, but you love her right now. Yes, I do!

After eating our lunches, I asked to speak with the manager. Pete came over and asked how he could help us.

"Well, I want to put together an impromptu party in about two weeks. I'm thinking, the 22nd or maybe sooner," I explained.

"Two weeks?" Pete asked astonishingly. "That's a little less notice than we usually ask for. We like to have at least a month's notice for catering. What's the occasion?"

Can't wait to see the look on his face in about three seconds.

"I'm dying. I have less than a month to live, and I want to have a going away party for my family and friends," I said straight-faced.

Yep, his face just dropped.

He looked at me to see if I was going to burst out into laughter. I mean, I had to be joking, right? When Pete noticed that I didn't break out into a smile, he let out a sorrowful sigh.

"Oh." It was all Pete could say. He stared at me a little bit longer, still hoping I'd say that I was joking. "That's an interesting reason to have a party, to say the least. How many people are you planning on having at your party? What would you like the menu to be? We are more than happy to accommodate you. Let me go grab our catering menu and see what we can come up with."

Delores and I sat with Pete for over an hour going over the menu and details. Their barbeque beef brisket was to die for, and since I was dying what better option of meat to serve? I also decided on honey barbeque pulled pork, house salads, corn on the cob, green beans with bacon, cornbread, and mini apple pies for dessert. With the menu, time, and catering details in place, Delores and I headed back home.

"Delores, before you leave, can you sit with me while I call Hospice care? I just don't want to be alone when I make the appointment for them to come out and set things up."

"Of course, Edna," she said. "I will do whatever you need me to do. I want to help in any way I can."

"Thanks, Delores. I needed to hear that. I need someone I can vent to and break down in front of other than the kids and mom. I just can't be strong for them every single step of the way."

DAY FOUR

"You have cancer. Cancer. Cancer."

I kept hearing the words over and over in my head. I rolled over to see the clock. It was just past 11 a.m. Didn't sleep in too late this time. Lots to do.

Hospice is coming at 1 o'clock this afternoon so you better get yourself up and ready. Do I have to? I mean, come on, don't dying people get to lay around in their pajamas with messed up hair and bad breath? You can if you want to, but you won't. You're right, I won't. Have you smelled my morning breath? Yes, it would kill a goat!

I walked into the kitchen and started the coffee. I had enough left to last the month. Good, I don't want to go to the grocery store. *You could stock up on stuff for when people are here cleaning out the house. That's not a bad idea. Let's make a list. Put snacks on the list; everyone wants snacks.*

I sat down at the table with my coffee in hand and started writing out the grocery list. I had about 20 items on the list. Staring at the list, I started to get angry.

Why the hell am I making a damn grocery list for other people? These leaches are going to be coming into my house, picking through my stuff, and deciding whether it is worth something or not. They'll be eating my food and drinking my drinks. They'll probably be discussing among themselves all the quirky things and talking about me. Why am I doing this?

I picked up the half-drank cup of coffee and threw it across the dining room. It hit the wall opposite where I was sitting and shattered. The coffee dripped down the wall making a pattern on the paint as it hit the floor. I stared at the pattern. It looked like one of those Rorschach tests. *Looks like a pelvis. You think they all look like a pelvis.*

I sat there staring at the pelvis coffee stain and started to cry. *Again, with the crying? I AM ALLOWED TO CRY! I don't want to die! I want to see my grandchildren grow up! I don't want to leave my children! I don't want to leave my garden! I don't want someone else living in my house! I don't want someone giving all my clothes away! I just don't want to die!*

The overwhelming enormity of it all came crashing down on me. I sat there for what seemed to be hours just crying.

Get up! Get some more coffee. It's cold by now. Heat it! That's why God invented the microwave. Gross. The coffee creamer gets all funky if it's microwaved. Then just heat it on the stove! Fine.

The doorbell rang at exactly 1 o'clock. Did they just sit in the car timing it out to arrive at the exact time of the appointment? *Probably. You do it all the time. Yes, but only because I am always way too early!*

"Mrs. Berman?" An extremely large, woman of medium height asked. I guessed her to be around 40-something. She had short blonde hair and a stiff demeanor.

"It's Ms." I corrected. Why does every person think a woman over a certain age has to be married?

"I'm sorry, *Ms.* Berman. My name is Judy, and I will be your hospice caretaker."

"Come on in," I told Judy. "Let's sit in the dining room. Can I get you something to drink?"

"Do you have iced tea or maybe some bottled water?"

Do you want a damn menu, too?

I put some ice in a glass and poured Judy some iced tea and set it in front of her. *She's lucky that iced tea is a must-have drink in the south!* I sat down in the chair opposite her.

Judy pulled out some paperwork that needed to be signed. "You'll need to fill these out while I'm here, so we have them on file. From my conversation with Dr. Linder, it looks like you will need our services starting immediately."

I thought Dr. Linder wanted you to call them. That bastard took all my thunder.

"When you say 'immediately' what does that mean?" I asked.

"We will set up an area in your home, and I will be coming here every day until the end to help with any medicine you will need to keep you comfortable and to keep a watch on you. It's all routine."

Where's Delores? She was supposed to be here by now.

I could feel myself start to panic. The reality was starting to kick in, and I wasn't handling it very well inside.

"What kind of medicine? I'm not in any pain at the moment. Why do you need to start immediately?" I fired off the questions.

"*Ms.* Berman," Judy emphasized the Ms., "I know this is all so sudden, but given the nature of your illness, the sooner we're here the better we can manage the time you have left. The pain will come, and you will need medication. Hospice is equipped to administer and monitor the amount of pain medication given. We're also equipped to help comfort family members and give guidance during your treatment. You or your family can add services such as light house cleaning or meal preparation as well." She stated emotionlessly.

The front door opened, and Delores came in. "Sorry, I'm late. What did I miss?"

You missed little Judy here telling me she's going to dope me up.

"Hi, I'm Judy. I'll be *Ms.* Berman's hospice nurse." She emphasized *Ms.* Again, "And, you are?"

"I'm Delores, Edna's neighbor, and best friend," Delores said so matter of fact that I saw Judy sit straight up as if Delores' statement offended her.

"Nice to meet you. We've just started going over the paperwork Ms. Berman needs to fill out, and then we'll decide where to set up the in-home treatment area."

Let's use the dining room table for my bed. Then no one will fight over it, and it can go to Goodwill. Who wants a table that someone died on, right? Yeah, imagine the next person who has the table, eating a nice fancy meal, maybe with their boss, seeing your ghost laying there!

Nurse Judy and I completed the necessary paperwork and decided to use the first-floor office as the setup area. She would return tomorrow with the bed, linens, and equipment necessary to make my last days as comfortable as possible. She would also bring the list of additional services for me to look over and decide if I wanted any.

After she left, I asked Delores why she was late.

"I drove downtown to Packard Street and got something for us." She stated with a mischievous grin.

"Packard Street? That's a pretty dangerous area, Delores. What did you get?" I furrowed my brows in concern.

"This!" She said holding up a zip-lock sandwich bag halfway filled with marijuana. The dried green leaves shimmered in the plastic bag Delores proudly displayed in front of me.

"Oh, no you didn't!" I said excitedly, giggling like a little kid just given a huge bag of candy.

"Yep. Let's get stoned!" She said matter-of-factly and started opening the bag. She also picked up some roll papers at the local gas mart on the way over to my house.

Delores rolled each of us a joint, and we lit them. After about half an hour as the marijuana started to kick in, Delores started laughing. I looked over at her sitting on the couch. She was doubled over in laughter. She was laughing so hard that her face was red, and she couldn't breathe.

"What's so funny?" I asked.

"Do you remember that time you decided you wanted a sports car, and we rented that Mustang?"

At the mention of the memory, I grinned, my eyes twinkling in amusement. I knew what Delores was talking about and started to laugh out loud now too. I must have been going through some mid-life crisis at the time.

Delores and I had gone over to the car rental place and rented a cherry-red Mustang. It was beautiful. A powerful, beast of a car. It was a two-door coupe with a v-8 engine. I couldn't wait to get behind the wheel.

We drove around for a while before I decided I wanted to see how fast the car could go. We headed out to the highway. There was a ten-mile stretch of highway that no one really uses because it doesn't connect the outskirts of town to downtown.

As we merged onto the highway, I noticed that there were hardly any cars around. It was the middle of the day, so most people were at work. I gunned the engine, and the car took off. In a split second, or so it seemed, I was flying down the highway. I looked down at the speedometer and I was speeding along at about 95 miles per hour.

Delores and I were giddy with the speed, passing cars here and there. Then suddenly, I see something in the far distance sitting in the middle of the road. We were getting close to it very quickly. As soon as I registered it was a turtle, I hit the brakes.

At 90 plus miles an hour, I don't care what kind of brakes you have, the car does not stop on a dime. The car started pulling to the right and I had to hold the steering wheel with both hands to stop it from going into a tailspin. The turtle was getting closer and seemed not to care that its eminent death was upon it.

The car finally stopped within inches of the turtle. Cars behind us swerved to avoid a collision. Hearts pounding at our sudden stop and near smattering of a poor, innocent turtle, we got out of the car. Delores started waving at the few cars on the road, to go around us. I went over, picked up the turtle, and put it on the side of the road in the direction the little fellow was headed.

We got back into the car and pulled over to the shoulder so I could gather my thoughts and calm my nerves. My hands were shaking. Once my heart rate slowed to its normal pace, I put my foot on the gas pedal, steered the car over to the far-right lane, and got off at the next exit. I immediately drove to the rental agency and turned the car in. That was enough high-speed adventure for me.

By the time we replayed the story, each taking a part of it, and trying to tell what happened, my stomach was hurting from laughing so much.

"I'm getting hungry. Delores, do you want something to eat?" I asked.

"Sure. Let's order something in and see if there's a movie we can watch." Delores said still catching her breath from all the laughter.

"That's a perfect idea." I mused and let Delores take care of ordering the food.

DAY FIVE

"Ms. Berman?" Judy asked standing over my bed.

I must have given her the code to the house because there she was, in my house, in my upstairs bedroom acting as if she owned the damn place.

"What?" I retorted harshly.

"We're here to set up the treatment area." She said, not in the least phased by my tone.

"Fine. Shut the door when you're done." I said, rolled over, and ignored her. I looked around my room. I was going to have to move downstairs now. I was going to have to give up the bedroom that I made mine over the years.

After the divorce, Russell didn't take too much of the furniture in the house. We split things up by who needed what the most. I didn't need the bedroom set and had told him I'd just use the spare room set until I got another set. I spent months looking for the perfect set. I wanted all the pieces to match. I had been into the farmhouse style, a style Russell never took to, so our mutual furniture was never to my liking anyway.

I had splurged some on the furniture. A lot more than I probably should have, but just coming out of a divorce, I treated myself. I bought another queen-size bed since I wasn't ready for any type of relationship. So, what was the sense of having something bigger?

It was a platform bed with storage drawers at the foot of the bed. It was a white shaker style. I bought a dresser, a chest of drawers, and a matching nightstand. I loved it.

Now I was going to have to move into a smaller room with just my dresser and nightstand to hold my belongings; clothes and such, that I would need for the next month or so. I was going to have to sleep in an antiseptic bed designed to be nurse-accessible and probably with a waterproof covering in the event of bodily accidents. The mere thought of it depressed me so much that I just turned to my side and made myself sleep away the daunting upcoming change of scenery.

DAY SIX

What the hell is all that banging? Jesus Christ! You're going to wake the dead!

"Mom?" It was Amelia. "I forgot the code." She yelled as she continued to bang on the door.

"I'm coming," I yelled back a little too nastily.

"Hi, Mom!" Amelia hugged me as she came through the door. "I brought over the party stuff. The Halloween stuff wasn't out yet, so I couldn't find any tombstones to decorate the place with."

Ah, that's my girl. Keeping it real.

"That's okay. What did you end up getting?" I asked curiously. My mood instantly lightened.

Amelia proceeded to empty all the party store bags onto the dining room table. "I got cups, two sizes of plates: one for the meal and one size for the dessert. I was thinking of going over to Granny's Bakery and ordering a cake. What size do you think we should get?"

"Oh, I don't know. Maybe enough for 20 people?" I guessed.

"Okay. I'll order that tomorrow. Have you decided on a date yet?" She asked.

No. Ryan Reynolds is still married and won't be able to make it. You go, girl, with your cougar self. Not that kind of date.

"I think I've decided on July 21st. I should still have some strength left until then." I said nonchalantly.

Amelia's face fell. She was trying to keep things light, but that little piece of information brought reality back into play.

"Oh. Good point." She whispered.

"What else did you buy at the store? Do you need any money?" I said, guiding the conversation away from the thoughts I knew were going through Amelia's head.

"No, Mom. I've got this. I also bought some black streamers, black Solo cups, and black napkins. They didn't have any black silverware, so I just got clear. Is that okay?"

"That's perfect, honey. Good job. I know it wasn't easy for you to do all that." I said looking around at all the party paraphernalia.

"It's okay, Mom. I was happy for the distraction if you want to call it that." She said as she fumbled to put all of the party stuff back into the bags.

"Hey, sweetie, while you're here, can you let me know what you would like of mine? I'm going to make a list and then anything left, you and Kevin can just donate to the Veterans Home."

"I don't want anything, Mom," she said looking at me as if I slapped her with reality.

"Honey, this has to be done, and I'd rather do it while I'm still somewhat sane." I tried to implore the necessity of sorting out my belongings before I was no longer able to do so.

"What's that smell?" Amelia sniffed in the air. "It smells like weed."

"Busted... well, yeah, that," I said like a teenage boy caught with his dad's Playboy magazine. "Delores is helping me with my appetite and weed gives me the munchies," I said sheepishly.

"That woman is crazy, mom." She laughed.

And a big help.

"She's a good friend, and she's keeping my spirits up." I chuckled.

"How are you feeling today, Edna?" Judy asked coming through the front door.

Who gave her a key? You don't have keys anymore, remember? Oh, yeah. Why is she calling me Edna? What happened to Ms. Berman? You told her to call you Edna, probably so she stopped emphasizing Ms. Oh, that's right.

"I'm feeling like a million bucks, Judy," I said sarcastically.

I don't like her. Why? Because she reminds me every day that I'm going to die, that's why. It's her job. Call her Nurse Death. No. Although... "I'm in a little pain today, Judy. I think I may have coughed up some blood last night too." I watched for her reaction.

"I'll take care of it for you. Do you want a Percocet or something stronger?" Judy questioned dryly.

Still a robot, void of emotion.

"Nothing, right now. Let me finish with my daughter, and maybe I'll take something afterward."

"I can leave, Mom, if you want to lay down and rest." Amelia volunteered. She didn't mention the blood though I was sure she heard the comment.

"No, honey, let's get this list done. I'll have Kevin come over later and let me know what he wants too."

Amelia and I went upstairs to my bedroom. I hadn't cleaned in there recently since I'd been falling asleep relatively early, and my room looked a mess. They had already taken my dresser and my nightstand downstairs. I'd be moving downstairs permanently in the next day or so.

"Sorry about the mess. You know I usually make up the bed and put the clothes away. I've just been feeling a little lazy, and they took some of the furniture downstairs, as you can see. I didn't see a point in keeping this too clean. I probably should though so you don't have to clean it later." I rambled on aimlessly trying to make a point.

"It's okay, Mom." Amelia was looking sad again. I couldn't help what she was feeling. I needed to get this done and now was a good time.

We sat in the room for a while going over my jewelry and personal belongings. Amelia decided on my diamond earrings and broach that Russell had given me for our fifth wedding anniversary.

"What are you going to do with all these albums?" She asked after finding my collection. Amelia took after me in her taste in music. We loved the heavy metal rock bands of the 80s and 90s and even some of the early 70s disco music. Neither one of us liked what they called music today. It was too auto-tuned and passionless.

"You can have them all if you want. Take the turntable too so you have something to play them on. Instead of giving what you don't want away, see about selling them on eBay. I'm sure some of them are worth a few bucks. Buy Henry something with the money you get."

We finished going through what Amelia wanted, and she even set aside some stuff that she thought Kevin would want for Gracie. My old ballet shoes, which were in good shape, she could grow into. Gracie loved to dance, and Kevin mentioned enrolling her in dance lessons next year. It would take her years to grow into those shoes, but maybe she could hang them in her room for inspiration.

After Amelia left, I asked Judy to leave. She gave me a Percocet, and when she left, I called Delores to come over. We lit up another joint, and between the pot and Percocet, I was feeling good. Delores left me sleeping on the couch and locked the door as she headed home. I hadn't called Kevin.

DAY SEVEN

"I don't want to do this, Mom," Kevin complained. He had come over after his conversation with his sister about going through my stuff to decide what he wanted for himself or what he thought should be donated to charity. He was the oldest, so I had burdened him with the responsibility of not only clearing out the house of my belongings but also being the executor of my will. It would fall on him to sell the house and my car; my only things of any real value, and to disperse any remaining money to himself, Amelia, and his grandmother.

"It must be done. I don't want you to decide two months after I'm gone that you wanted something of mine, and it's now with a Veteran who wouldn't understand the sentimental value."

"Fine." Kevin got frustrated with me. But I knew the frustration was coming from the emotional pain he was feeling.

Kevin made a list of what he wanted. He decided on some rare classic books that I picked up at yard sales over the years, some gold necklaces that he thought Paula would like, and of course, the ballet shoes for Gracie. "I've got to go pick up Gracie from daycare. When's the party?" he said hurriedly. I knew that what I put him through today was getting too much for him to bear a minute more.

"It's the 21st. I'm thinking around 6 o'clock. That way people can eat and stay a bit but leave before I'm too tired," I said, trying to cheer him up.

"Sounds great, Mom. I'll see you before then, I just wanted to know when and what time so Paula and I can get a sitter. Is there anything you need before I leave? Can I fix you something to eat?"

Just your time, son. A hug would be nice too.

"No, honey. Nurse Death is downstairs, and she'll fix me something to eat." *She always makes me eat.* "By the way, thanks for adding meal prep and cleaning services to the hospice care. That will help me out a lot."

"I'm happy to make things easier for you, Mom." Kevin came over to me and hugged me. I could feel his body starting to shake with emotion. He pulled away and kissed me. "I love you, Mom." He said, quickly turning away to leave, so I wouldn't see the tears build in his eyes.

Judy came upstairs about ten minutes later. I was on the phone with Karen.

"Hang on for a second, Karen." I turned to Judy and said, "Yes?"

"Would you like me to fix you some lunch?" she asked.

"That would be nice. Thank you." I said dismissively. Judy turned and headed back downstairs.

"Sorry about that, Karen," I said returning to my phone conversation.

"I don't know what to say, Edna," Karen had seen the post on social media about my ending endeavor party that Amelia created as an event. Karen and I worked together at the bank for a few years before I decided to retire early.

"It's okay, Karen. I know it's a shock to a lot of people, including myself. Please don't feel obligated to come. It's just a small get-together for one last hoorah if you'd like, so I can say my goodbyes and maybe share a laugh or two."

"I'll be there. I wouldn't miss it for the world. I need a big hug from you!" Karen was the office hugger. She was also very dramatic about everything.

"Thanks, Karen. I look forward to seeing you again. You take care." I hung up the phone.

"Judy?" I asked as I walked downstairs into the kitchen where Judy was finishing up lunch preparations.

"Do you think you could give me one of those pain pills? I'm not feeling very good and my side hurts."

Judy stopped what she was doing and asked me to come into the office bedroom. Judy made me sit on the bed. She took her stethoscope out and listened to my chest and heart rate. Then she checked the strength in my arms.

"Push down on my arms." She said as she laid her forearms under my forearms. I started to push down when a sharp pain shot through my ribs.

"Ouch. That hurts!" I exclaimed.

"That's the cancer entering into your bones." She had a look on her face of pity.

I'm going to slap her; I swear to God if she doesn't stop looking at me like that. It's called empathy, you twit. No, it's not. She doesn't have any emotions.

"Would you like something stronger for the pain?" She asked.

"Yes, I think I would. Thank you," I replied.

Judy had me lie down on the bed. She took my shoes off. I was suddenly very cold. She must have anticipated I would be and had brought in a blanket for me.

"I'm just going to give you a little shot of morphine for the pain. It will work better than Percocet. Since you've reached this stage, I'm going to have to call in 24-hour care because you will be out of sorts when the morphine kicks in." Judy informed me.

Great! More strangers in my house. How are Delores and I going to sneak off?

"Hey, Judy? Can you call my mom? I know she's been worried about me, and I'd like to see her soon." My words were starting to slur.

"Sure thing, Ms. Berman. I mean, Edna." She said apathetically.

Don't forget to water the plants. *Did you say that out loud? I think so. They do need to be watered. But you don't have any plants. Oh okay, well I hope I didn't say that out loud then.*

DAY EIGHT

"Hey there, sleepy head."

Is that Mom? What's on top of me that's so damn heavy? I think it's a blanket.

I slowly opened my eyes. My mouth was dry, like cotton stuck on my tongue. I smacked my lips and tried to get the word *"water"* out, pulling the blanket off my head.

"Wa-er." I couldn't make the "t" because my tongue was stuck to the roof of my mouth. Mom must have realized what I was trying to say, and she left. When she returned, she had a glass of water. I drank the entire glass, then set the empty glass down on the table next to the bed.

"What time is it?" I asked.

"It's seven-ten. Are you hungry?" Mom responded. No wonder I'm hungry: I must have slept all afternoon.

"Do we have any fried chicken?" I asked as I started to sit up.

"You want fried chicken for breakfast?" Mom asked with a puzzled look on her face.

"Breakfast?" Now I was puzzled.

"Yes, Honey, you slept all day yesterday. I can fix you fried chicken if you want. I may have to go to the store. Caroline is here and she can watch you while I'm gone."

Okay. You need to wake up and focus. Who's Caroline?

"Who's Caroline, Mom?" I inquired.

"Oh, she's one of the new nurses. When Judy called me yesterday as you asked her to, she explained that since you're now on morphine, they need to have round-the-clock nurses here to watch over you. Judy said that Caroline will be your midnight to 8 a.m. nurse, Judy will take the 8:00 AM to 4:00 PM shift, and then a young man named Jonathan would be here the third shift from 4:00 PM until midnight."

Mom left to start putting some breakfast together for us. The smell of food cooking came into my room and my stomach growled. I started thinking about what she had just told me about the round-clock additional nurses.

Jonathan? I have a male nurse. That's interesting. Oh, Delores is not going to like Caroline! It's not THE Caroline. I know, but the poor creature just happened to have that name.

"Breakfast is ready, Edna," Mom called from the kitchen.

I went into the dining room just as she was placing a plate down for me. *Wow! Where did she find all this stuff?*

"Looks good, Mom. Thank you." I said.

I sat down at the table just staring at the food as if I had no idea what to do next.

"Thanks, Honey. Now eat," she commanded.

"How are you feeling today?" Mom inquired cautiously.

"Aside from a little bit of pain, I guess I'm doing okay." *Liar! A little bit of pain my ass. You had enough morphine in you to knock out an elephant. She doesn't need to know that.* "I think I want to go fishing today with Delores," I said quickly changing the subject.

"Fishing? You don't know the first thing about fishing." She looked astonished.

"You put a worm on a hook and throw it into the water. How hard can that be, Mom?" I quipped.

"Okay, okay," she said, a little taken aback. "Whatever you want to do is fine with me. I'm going to stick around and help you clean up this place a little bit."

Yes, Mom. I've been a slob, I know. Please make me feel like I'm six again with a messy room. Stop it. Let her clean up if she wants. I have a cleaning person coming regularly now, thanks to Kevin. So what? She needs to feel useful, and you know it. I know, I know. Again, I'm sorry for my sarcastic attitude. No, you're not.

I called Delores and asked her to come over in an hour and bring Harold's fishing poles. She was a little surprised at the request but said she'd do so anyway. Harold didn't even get his fishing poles in the divorce.

"Who's up for some fishing?" Delores asked with a bright, fake smile as she came through the door.

"Oh. Hi, Mrs. Slater," Delores said after noticing my mom dusting the end tables.

"Hi, Delores. I understand you and Edna are going fishing today. Just don't keep her out too long," Mom said with a concerned look on her face, and you could tell she wasn't too happy about Delores and me going out in the heat just to catch a fish and throw it back into the water.

"Let's go," I said, and out the door, we went. I didn't need to hear the scolding.

Delores lives close enough to the water and was friends with a lady who had access to a pier. Delores said she asked if we could use the pier for the day and was granted permission to do so. As we sat on the pier and started putting the bait on the hooks, Delores looked over at me.

"Why did you want to go fishing today, Edna?" Delores queried.

"I don't know. I remember when Russell and I were married, and he'd go on weekend fishing trips with his buddies. He always came back in a great mood, so I thought maybe I'd try it, too," I shrugged.

"But you don't like fish," Delores said observantly.

"I know. I'm not going to eat them. I just want to catch one and then put it back," I smiled at her.

"Okay. We can do that," she giggled.

We sat there for a while with our fishing lines just lying in the water. It was a clear day. It was not too hot outside, which was always a plus for Louisiana weather. It was, however, muggy, and I had to wipe the sweat off my forehead now and then.

Occasionally, the fishing lines would get a little twitch, but no fish hooked onto the bait. I watched as the bobber bounced gently up and down in the water, luring the fish to their ultimate death. I imagined the fish, mindlessly swimming along and then suddenly discovering something floating beneath the surface, in their underwater world, that resembled food. At least enough to tempt them to taste it and then, BAM! They were locked in a fierce battle with the spiked hook that caught them on the side of their cheek. Flailing back and forth trying to lose the hook. Feeling the tug of some strange force pulling it closer and closer to the surface. Gasping at the air, instead of water, that now filled its lungs.

My mind then drifted to other thoughts as I gazed out at the calm waters, staring at the still fishing lines, bouncing bobber luring the unsuspecting fish.

I should take Gracie and Henry fishing one day. They would get a kick out of trying to bait the hook. Oh, the joy they would have on their little faces if they caught a fish! Gracie would probably scream with delight! I'm going to miss them growing up.

"What are you thinking about?" Delores' question brought me back to the present situation.

"I was just thinking about Gracie and Henry. I'm going to miss them so much, Delores. I'm going to miss the milestones like graduations and weddings, but more importantly, I'm going to miss the little things. I will miss the scrapped knees, the pumpkin carvings, the joy of opening Christmas presents, birthdays, and

Fourth of July fireworks." My voice started to crack. "Will you tell them all about me when I'm gone so they don't forget about me?" The words caught in my throat.

Delores put her arm around my shoulder and hugged me. "Of course, I will, Sweetie. Of course, I will."

I sat there and let Delores hug me. She didn't know what to say to me, so she didn't say anything. She just comforted me, gently rocking me sideways with her as we sat on the pier.

"This is boring as shit, you know," I said shaking off my pensive mood after a minute or two.

"You're right about that. Want to do something else?" Delores asked hopefully.

"Not today. I'm getting a little tired. I think I should head on back to the house. Maybe I'll sit and read a bit and just relax."

You can relax anytime in about three weeks. Do something! Stay outside. Enjoy the fresh air. Go for a walk!

"On second thought. How about we go for a walk on the beach for a bit?" I suddenly asked.

Delores was a little surprised at my change in plans. "That sounds like a wonderful idea. Let me put the poles away, and I'll come right back." Delores turned and headed towards her house.

When Delores came back, we jumped down off the pier and walked along the beach. She didn't ask me any questions. She just walked beside me. Sometimes she would point to a shell laying on the sand or comment about a boat or two in disrepair alongside some of the dilapidated piers.

I took off my sandals and felt the gritty sand on the bottom of my feet. The sand was hot, so I walked along the water's edge feeling the cool water wash over my feet. The small waves ebbed and flowed bringing wetness to the sand only to take it back out again. The humidity was negated by the cool breeze coming off the water. I took in the smells surrounding me. The water had a distinct smell. The smell was a combination of moisture, dead fish, and seaweed. It filled my nostrils and cleared my mind better than any meditation device. I closed my eyes, and I took it all in.

"I think I'd like to head back home now, Delores, if you don't mind," I said tiredly.

Delores took me home, and I told her I'd call her later in the week. I walked through the front door to find mom sitting on the couch. She looked a little tired, and I knew immediately that she outdid herself cleaning up the house. I sat down next to her and put my head on her shoulder. It was a type of bonding moment that daughters and mothers can feel in their bones.

"I love you, Mom," I whispered.

She turned her face and kissed me on my head. "I love you, too, Honey."

We stayed in that position for a few minutes just being close to one another. I took in a deep breath and sat up.

"Thanks for helping today with the cleaning, Mom. I really appreciate it. I don't think I can do much on my own, so your being here to help with the house makes things a little easier for me. I think I'm going to lay down for a bit though if you don't mind. All that sunshine and fresh air have made me tired."

"I don't mind at all, honey. You get some rest. I'll stop by again soon." She said and started gathering up her things to leave.

After she left, I went into the makeshift hospital room and laid down on the bed. Judy came in and gave me a shot of the morphine I asked for. It wasn't very long before I was sound asleep.

DAY NINE

The phone was ringing. I tried to get my sleepy body out of bed in time before the answering machine picked up the call. Too late.

"Yes, I will let her know. Thank you for calling." I heard Caroline say. *It must be before 8 AM.*

I stumbled into the living room still in my pajamas. *I'm glad you brought those downstairs. Strangers don't need to be seeing your naked ass just because that's the way you prefer to sleep.*

"Who was on the phone, Caroline?" I asked hesitantly at her name. It was the first time I was able to put a face with the name.

Caroline looked nothing like Harold's Caroline. She was a heavy-set black woman who reminded me of Octavia Spencer. Her dark blue nurse's uniform fit a little snug for her, but she had the most beautiful smile known to man. Her very aura instantly brought peace to me, and I knew that I was in good, caring hands with this woman.

"It was your son, Kevin, ma'am." She said, bringing me out of my trance. "He asked that you give him a call when you woke up."

"Okay. Thank you." I said. "Caroline?" I added.

"Yes, ma'am?" She inquired as she turned to me.

"Thank you for watching over me at night." I choked up as her peace aura filled me and the words were raspy as they found their way out of my mouth.

"You are most welcome, Miss Edna." She smiled.

"Please, just call me Edna." I smiled back.

I dialed Kevin's phone number as I sat on the couch and waited for him to answer.

"Hey, Kev. Sorry, I just missed your call. I heard the phone ringing, but I couldn't get to it in time."

"No worries, Mom. I just wanted to try to catch you early in the day. I hope I didn't wake you up."

"No, you didn't wake me." *Liar!* "I'm quite surprised that I am up this early though." *Oh, that's a good one. It had nothing to do with the phone ringing you out of your overtime slumbering.* "I've been sleeping in late in the mornings. What did you need?" I asked.

"I don't need anything, Mom. I spoke with Amelia last night and we thought that maybe you'd like for Gracie and Henry to come over for a couple of hours either today or tomorrow." His voice was a little shaky, and I knew it was because he was trying to say that I should spend some time with my grandchildren before I didn't have the strength to, and he didn't want to say the words he was thinking.

"That is a wonderful idea, Kevin. How about you bring them over tomorrow? I went fishing with Delores yesterday, and I don't think I have the strength to do much else today other than sit on the couch and watch some television. I should be better tomorrow. You can bring them over around 10 AM."

"That sounds good, Mom. I'll bring them over and then pick them up around 2 PM. I don't want you to overexert yourself." He said somewhat concerned.

"Sounds like a plan. I'll see you tomorrow." I hung up the phone and sat down on the couch.

Overexert myself, huh? Four hours of grandkid time, and he thinks I'm going to be too tired for more. *He's right, you know. I know, I just don't want to admit it.*

The time is ticking away way too quickly. Can it slow down just for one day so I can enjoy my grandchildren and build some sort of memories for them to hold on to?

DAY TEN

At a few minutes 'til 10 the next day, Henry and Gracie came bounding through the front door with Kevin in tow carrying two backpacks stuffed with toys and games.

"Grammy!" Gracie said skipping over to hug me. I kissed her smiling face and cheeks. She smelled like she had just washed her hair with strawberry shampoo. It was such a sweet scent, and I stood there for a moment reveling in her hugs and fragrance.

Henry wasn't going to let his older cousin have all the kisses. He wedged his way in between us calling out, "Gammy, Gammy, Gammy". Two-year-olds just can't quite get the "r" in words.

I sat there letting my grandchildren hug and kiss me for as long as their attention span would allow. I didn't want them to stop, and I always let them pull away first. Gracie was the first to stop hugging me, but Henry sat on my lap giggling as I now had the space to tickle him. Eventually, I got him out of my lap, and I stood up. I walked over to Kevin and hugged him also.

"Hi, Sweetie. Thanks for bringing them over. What a joy they are to me." I said a little out of breath but so happy in the moment. "What's in their bags?" I asked.

"In Gracie's bag, there are some Barbie dolls, coloring books, crayons, and some type of wooden craft that, I think, is to be made into an airplane. Henry has some new cartoon figurines, a couple of toy trucks and cars, and lots of diapers. It should be enough to keep them, and you, occupied for a couple of hours." Kevin relayed the contents of each child's belongings.

"Amelia also asked me to remind you that Henry needs to take his chewy vitamin. He didn't want Amelia to give it to him when he found out he was coming to see you." Kevin chuckled.

"He's such a sweetheart," I said grinning a little.

Boys always have a special place in a mother's and grandmother's hearts. Don't get me wrong: I love my granddaughter to pieces. Gracie and I have a different, special bond along the lines of best friends who can talk about anything. She's my go-to when I want to talk about life and dreams of the future. Boys? They don't get too emotional and don't think about anything beyond the present. They live for today's mischief in an endearing kind of way.

"Well, call me if you need a bailout sooner than 2 PM. I took today off work to get some work done on the bathroom Paula wants to have updated. She's finally decided on the faucet fixtures. I plan on installing them today, and I'm going to pick up the paint color she picked out on my way home." With that, Kevin gave me a hug and kiss, told Gracie to behave herself, tussled Henry's hair, and left.

"What do you two want to do today?" I asked, clapping my hands in excitement.

"I want to play Barbies and color," Gracie spoke up first.

"Tucks and cars!" Henry shouted. "I wanna play tucks."

"Well, how about you find your trucks in your bag, Henry, and we'll put them on the table." I emphasized the "r" in trucks in the hopes that he would start using the proper pronunciation.

Henry immediately turned and went over to his backpack. It was a bright blue with some sort of spaceship on the front flap. He started rummaging through the bag looking for his toys, pulling out all his diapers first, tossing them sporadically on the floor behind him as if the thought of diapers made him feel like he was still a baby.

I turned to Gracie and said, "Let's get Henry started on his trucks and play with him for a little while before he lays down for his nap.

Then you and I can have some girl time to color or play with your Barbies. How does that sound?" I plotted with her in a secretive girl-to-girl fashion.

Gracie was reluctant to play trucks, but she realized that when Henry was taking his nap, she could have me all to herself, so she agreed.

Henry grabbed a yellow excavator truck with a scooper on the front of it that moved up and down and a red race car that sort of resembled a mustang. I gave a little smile when he proudly showed it to me. He sat at the dining room table holding one toy in each hand.

"Voom, voom." He kept saying as he rolled their tires up and down his arm's length on the table. Now and then, he would release the race car, and it would roll over to Gracie. She would attempt some sort of car sound and send it rolling back to him. He would giggle and vroom, vroom some more.

Gracie had pulled out her coloring book and crayons. She was old enough to now have a 32-count box of crayons. To her, they were so much more mature than the 8-pack she had when she was Henry's age. She quietly sat at the table coloring a flower that looked like a giant daisy. Very meticulously, she would press down a crayon on the outline to make the color darker than the space she would fill in with the same color. She would aimlessly send Henry's trucks back to him if he pushed them her way.

I watched them play at the table. Occasionally, I would remark on Gracie's coloring or pass the truck or car back to Henry when he pushed them over to me. I just reflected on every single facial expression they made at their tasks. I watched Gracie furrow her brow when she was concentrating on making sure the crayon didn't leave its track around each flower petal. She would scrunch over to see the outline better and when she finished outlining a petal, she would sit up and examine it. Then, she would scrunch over again to color the inside of the lines.

Henry would make car and truck sounds. Sometimes he would make screeching tire sounds. Sometimes he would make car horn beeping sounds. He would crash the excavator truck and car together and then blow air out of his mouth like a crashing sound. When he got too loud, Gracie would politely ask him to keep his voice down. He would say "Okay, Gacie" and lower his voice while continuing to make all the sounds.

I took it all in. My heart started to feel as if there was a vice grip tightening it. My shoulders started to drop, and I could feel the tears welling up in my eyes. My precious grandchildren. I loved them so much, and it hurt deeply knowing I wasn't going to be around for them. I wanted to see them grow up. I wanted to be in their lives celebrating their accomplishments. I wanted my living room filled with milestone pictures of t-ball, ballet lessons, Boy Scouts, and proms. I wanted them to remember me. I knew that only Gracie would have a vague memory of me as she grew older. Henry's memory would be formed solely from the stories his mom, aunt, and uncle would tell him. He wouldn't have a concrete memory of me.

I didn't want the grandkids to see me in this state, so I stood up and asked, "Who wants some lunch?"

I had turned towards the kitchen so they couldn't see my face before I was able to wipe my tears on the kitchen towel hanging from the stove handle.

"Me!" Both Gracie and Henry exclaimed together.

"Great!" I said, turning around and smiling. "I'll make some peanut butter and jelly sandwiches with some apple slices. How does that sound?"

"Good!" They both said in unison.

I made the sandwiches, sliced up some apples after taking the skin off them, and poured some grape juice into glasses. When I brought the food over to each of them, they put what they were working on to the side and waited for me to bring my plate over to the table. When I sat down, they folded their hands together waiting for me to say grace. I was a little shocked that Henry did this as I was sure Amelia was angry with God. Amelia was always angry with God every time something happened that she felt was unfair in life. I was sure my diagnosis added to her list. Apparently, though, she still gave Him thanks for the food.

Gracie started talking about school coming up next month. She was excited to start second grade because she didn't want to be in the first grade anymore. She was so much older than the kids in the first grade, and they were just babies in her eyes. Luckily, Henry didn't understand her meaning when she was calling kids only one grade behind her 'babies.' I just chuckled at her statement and told her how proud I was of her and that I hoped she was going to have a great school year.

Henry started rubbing his eyes, and I knew it was getting close to nap time. Before he finished his grape juice, I handed him his chewy vitamin. He chewed it up and washed it down with the remaining juice. I took the dishes over to the kitchen and placed them in the sink. I'd wash them later. Or Judy would.

"Gracie, would you mind if I took Henry upstairs to the bedroom so he could take a nap?" I asked, winking.

Knowing that we would have our time together after I came downstairs, she graciously agreed. Henry held my hand, and we went upstairs to the spare bedroom. I asked if he needed to potty. When he didn't answer me, I knew it was too late. I changed his diaper and helped him up onto the bed. I brought an Afghan blanket over from the old cedar chest at the end of the bed to cover him up. I laid down with him, and he snuggled up to me laying his head on my stomach. He giggled a little when he told me that my stomach was making noise. I stroked his thick, dark hair. He must have inherited his hair from Tony. It only took a few minutes before I could tell he was asleep. He never did fight sleep like most toddlers.

As he lay there, head on my stomach, peacefully sleeping, I wanted to just go to sleep with him. There's such a sense of calmness and serenity when a child is sleeping next to you. You know they have no cares in the world and trust you emphatically enough to just fall asleep knowing they're safe. I stayed in that peace for a few more minutes before I slowly rolled out from under his head, placing it gently on the bed. I needed to get down to Gracie who would be impatiently waiting for me.

I came down the stairs to find that Gracie had taken out the wooden airplane craft and placed it on the table.

"I think you're too old for Barbies, so I got the plane out for us to do," she said sounding so grown up.

"Oh, you think I'm old, huh?" I winked at her.

Before she realized the error of her words, I walked over and hugged her to me. "It's okay, Sweetie. I'm never too old for you."

Gracie and I set out to color the plane first before we glued it together. I watched in amazement as she crafted the pieces of wood into a beautiful biplane. She picked the perfect colors of red and yellow for the body, blue for the wings, and a touch of black for the tail fin.

While she was putting the plane pieces together, she told me of a new friend she made at school. Her name was Shelly, and she had just moved into her neighborhood. She was going to have a sleepover with her next month, and they were going to have a princess party. Shelly's mom worked at the party store and could get all the decorations they needed for half off. I don't think Gracie knew exactly what that meant other than the fact Shelly's mom would be able to get a lot of princess stuff for the party.

Gracie's pure innocence made me smile and remember Amelia at her age, bouncing from one thought to the other with hardly a pause between them. Both my grandchildren reminded me of my children. Some little facial expressions or the way they moved their hands when they talked or the way they walked. It amazed me how these traits get handed down through the generations.

Before I knew it, Kevin was coming through the front door. I turned and looked at the clock. I guess I thought he was early. Surely four hours hadn't passed that quickly. Kevin must have seen me look at the clock because he said, "Did I give you enough time, Mom?"

"I just didn't realize how much fun we all were having. I'll go get Henry up." I started to get up from the table.

"That's okay, Mom. I'll get him. He's probably still asleep so I'll just put him in his car seat without waking him," he said.

"Okay. That's probably a good idea. Gracie? Why don't you help me put everything away while your Dad is getting Henry?"

Gracie and I packed both backpacks with all their belongings while Kevin brought Henry down. He was still asleep, so I kissed his forehead as Kevin took him out to the car.

I hugged Gracie and held on to her until her father came back into the house.

"I had a good time today, Grammy," she said as she turned to leave with her dad.

"I did too, sweetie. I love you, and I'll see you soon." I said trying not to break down in front of her.

I waved to Kevin as he and Gracie walked out the door. I shut the door and turned to sit down on the couch. Judy came around the corner from wherever she was lurking during the visit.

"Yes, Judy. I need some medicine. Thank you." I turned with Judy following me to the bedroom and laid down to rest for the remainder of the day.

Thirty Days Until I Die And Arguing With Myself About It

DAY ELEVEN

I woke up with a startle. My t-shirt was soaked in sweat, and I was breathing hard. It was dark with only the faint light of the living room lamp softly illuminating the corners of the downstairs rooms. I looked at the clock to see what time it was. It was 2:30 AM. I sat there recalling the dream I had just experienced.

The kids and I were taking a walk on the sidewalk of the neighborhood we lived in when Russell and I were still married. Russell wasn't walking with us.

Probably at work, as usual.

It was a crisp October mid-morning day; maybe 62 degrees and sunny. The changing leaves on the trees were almost at the end of their cycle. Many of the trees already were bare, but a few hung onto their vibrant reds and yellows.

The kids were chatting about a cat they saw running through the neighbor's yard. Everything seemed fine until it didn't. Suddenly, the air became extremely cold. It was as if the temperature had dropped twenty degrees. We started shivering as we only had light jackets on.

"Mommy, what's going on?" Kevin asked nervously. He and Amelia were holding hands, quickly looking all around them as if their names were being called from all directions.

"I'm not sure, Honey," I said with concern in my voice. I looked around the neighborhood. Everything seemed normal.

A few cars were parked in front of their respective houses. Leaves were scattered here and there making some green lawns look brown. The wind had picked up some of the leaves and was twirling them around the yards in little lawn tornados. The street noise itself seemed eerily quiet, but how often do you truly pay attention to every sound of the outside world? Then I saw it.

A black cloud appeared in the bright and sunny sky. It started descending, swirling around slowly at first, but then picking up speed until it was touching the pavement of our quiet little street. I remember feeling a tug at my jacket as if the cloud was pulling me towards it.

The kids started to scream "Mommy" in unison as my feet left the pavement, and I began floating toward the cloud. I could hear their screams fade further and further into the background as the force of the cloud pulled me closer and closer.

The temperature plummeted. It felt as if I was being pulled into a dark freezer. The closer I got, the colder I felt. The sound of the dark cloud filled my ears. It was as if I was in a wind tunnel. I couldn't stop the pull. I had no control over the situation. Just pulling. I stretched my arms out as if to stop myself from crossing into the cloud. My fingers felt the sting of ice, but I kept trying to push myself away from the cloud. I turned my face away as I reached the edge of the cloud; closing my eyes to shut out the sight of crossing into that dark abyss.

That's when I woke up.

What the hell was all that about? How should I know? Well, you were in the dream, too! It's probably the morphine making you have a vivid imagination. Yeah, well, it can stop anytime.

I laid my head back down on my pillow. I could hear Caroline quietly turning the pages of some magazine or book she must have been reading.

Sitting up in the middle of the night waiting for me to die must be boring as shit!

I was afraid to fall back asleep. Eventually, my body started to relax. I pulled the covers up to just under my chin. I felt cold even though it was a comfortable seventy-five degrees in the house. My mind started wondering if I'd see the dark, ominous cloud again. I knew, that if I closed my eyes, it would be there. The pull of sleep and morphine was too strong for me to stay awake any longer. My breathing slowed, my head sunk into my pillow, and I finally went back to sleep without stepping back into that dream where I was positive death was waiting for me on the other side.

DAY TWELVE

At 10:00 AM the next day, Delores came over. She walked through the door carrying a paper bag with handles that had the name of a store called "Puzzle Me This." I knew the place well. When the kids were younger, Russell and I would take them there for simple, wooden jigsaw puzzles. They seemed to always have the latest cartoon character sliced in 16-20 pieces large enough that a 3-year-old wouldn't choke on them. Amelia loved putting them together much more than Kevin did.

Kevin could never sit still long enough to put two end pieces together on the puzzle much less 16 of them.

Luckily, Delores did not have the latest cartoon character puzzle. *She must think you still have functioning brain cells that haven't quite diminished yet from your drug-induced pain relief.*

She pulled out a 1000-piece puzzle. As she pulled out the puzzle, she did so very slowly, with intention. It was a close-up of a seemingly flesh-colored mushroom growing wildly on a green forest floor. She looked me straight in the eye, daring me to say something about the provocative, painstakingly slow way she was removing the mushroom puzzle from the clutches of its bag.

"Delores, just pull the dick out!" I finally said rolling my eyes at her childishness.

It did seem a little tempting, didn't it? Shut up! Who's going to want to take a roll in the sack with someone drugged up on morphine and wouldn't be able to participate? Bill Cosby? Oh, no you didn't. I'm just thinking, haven't said a word. Besides, it's all over the TV. Hey, maybe Johnathon is into that kind of thing. He gets here at 4 o'clock today. Shut up, damn it!

Obviously, Delores didn't hear the conversation in my head. If she had, she would have added her two cents about the need for one last roll before I rolled over.

"You're too funny, Edna." She said laughing as she finally pulled the puzzle out and put it on the dining room table. "I thought we'd just sit here today and see how much of this puzzle we can get done. I heard the grandkids were over the other day, and you must still be a little tired from that."

"That's true. I wish I still had a fraction of their energy for just ten minutes a day." I replied wistfully.

"You and me both, sister!" Delores fired back jokingly.

We sat there not talking for a while. The only sound was the pieces of the puzzle being sorted through to find the edges and the sighs when what one of us thought was a matching piece didn't have the right locking components. Delores noticed that I wasn't in the mood for small talk. She always was able to sense when I just needed to be alone with my thoughts. She simply picked up pieces of the puzzle, tried to put them where she thought they should go, and let me do the same.

After about an hour of this, I looked over at Delores and said sheepishly, "Do you mind if we finish this up another time?"

"Of course not, Honey. Are you tired?"

"Yeah, just a little," I said.

I knew what Delores was thinking: what "another" time? She looked at me with what seemed akin to pity, but I knew Delores better than to pity me. She was trying to hold it all together. I could not imagine what she was going through. I had been selfish with my own thoughts and feelings, except for my immediate family, that it didn't occur to me that my best friend was also losing her best friend. And she was losing her much more quickly than she bargained for.

"I promise, Delores. We will finish the puzzle before... well, you know." I said quietly in an almost whisper.

"Okay, honey. I'm going to just leave the puzzle here. You can pick at it if you want now and then. When you're ready, just give me a ring, and we'll work on it some more." She said.

Delores turned to leave but not before she hugged me. Delores and I didn't hug regularly. It was just understood we loved each other; we didn't need an external show of affection to relay that. However, from time to time, some situation would come up where a hug was the most appropriate, and needed, thing in the world. Today was one of those situations.

I squeezed Delores in return. She headed towards the door. I could tell she was sorrowful. Her shoulders were slightly slumped, and she didn't turn back to me to say goodbye.

When she closed the door, I closed my eyes and tilted my head towards the ceiling letting out a long sigh.

Each day. Each good-bye. Each passing day was a little harder.

DAY THIRTEEN

Something woke me up. I turned to look at the clock. The bright red numbers illuminated the time: 2:13 AM. I laid there for a moment trying to figure out what aroused me from my sleep. Then I heard it. It was a soft humming sound coming from the living room.

It must be Caroline. What's that tune? I don't know. You're the music aficionado; you figure it out.

I laid there listening more intently to the rise and fall of the notes. At first, I thought it was just nonsense humming. There wasn't any structure to the tune. Then the notes began to come together, and I slowly recognized what Caroline was humming. She was humming an old Southern gospel spiritual called "Because He Lives." I hadn't heard that song in ages. I found myself starting to hum along, and that's when I decided to get up and go out into the living room for a chat with Caroline.

As I walked through the archway from the dining room into the living room, Caroline noticed me and stopped humming.

"Hello, Miss Edna. Is there something I can get you?" she asked.

Caroline had been knitting. She had completed several rows of a very pale blue project. When I had come into the living room, she set it aside.

"Hi, Caroline. No, thank you. I just woke up and heard you humming, and I thought I would come in to sit a bit if that's okay?" I replied.

"Oh, I'm very sorry that I disturbed you. I was just knitting, and well, the humming comes automatically. I apologize again, Ms. Edna," she said with concern.

"Please, Caroline, call me Edna," I said with a smile.

"Okay, ma'am. I will do my best, but that's hard for me to do given my upbringing and all."

"I understand, but you really don't have to call me Ms. Edna. If you don't mind, can I just sit and talk with you for a bit? When I first met you, there was something about your aura, for lack of a better word, that just resonated with me. It may sound foolish to you, but your spirit fills me with a sense of comfort and peace," I said as I sat down next to her on the couch.

"Thank you, Ms....., I mean, Edna," she stumbled, "That is a very nice thing to say to me. I try my best to comfort all my patients. I know that at this time in their life there is so much pain and anguish and, to an extent, some genuine fear. I've always felt it was my calling to comfort those who are getting ready to cross."

"Can you tell me a little bit about yourself, Caroline?" I asked somewhat sheepishly, but I truly wanted to know how this woman came to be so comforting.

You're getting really mushy here. Shut up. I'm scared, and I don't want anyone to know. She's calming, and I want to talk to her.

"Hmm, that's a little complicated, but I'll give it a go," she said.

I knew that she was going to tell me a story that would enrich the few days I had left on this Earth. Her voice itself brought me instant peace.

"I was born in Louisiana not far from here at the beginning of the 1960s. My momma was a maid for a very nice white couple who had two small children: a boy and a girl. She didn't help raise the children as you saw in that movie; she just cleaned their house. When she was at work, my oldest sister, Mabel, would watch me. Mabel would push me in my stroller in the mornings before it would get too hot. She would make my breakfast and lunches and play with me until momma got home. She'd also be my comfort when the weather would turn crazy, and we had to run into the cellar as the skies turned green." Caroline started.

"Mabel wanted to be a nurse. She would get old rags and bound them around my arms or legs like she was putting on a bandage. She would take my temperature with the back of her hand checking for any fever. She'd tell me that if I had a fever, then I would have an infection. We'd do this all summer long." Her story intrigued me, and I listened as she continued.

"Around the end of summer, just before school was getting ready to start, Mabel heard about a demonstration that would be going on in a place called Plaquemine. She had snuck out of the house and caught a bus to the town. She was big on the civil rights movements going on throughout the South. This was in 1963, and I was three years old. I don't know if you've heard about the Plaquemine riots, Edna. Many people haven't, but I will never forget what those riots did to my sister. Black folks were protesting when the police came in on mounted horses, driving the protesters away with tear gas and prods. It was like they were herding cattle. A lot of the protesters were driven into a Baptist church. That didn't seem to be enough just getting the protesters off the streets. The police then turned on the fire hoses and sprayed high-pressure water into that church. My sister got caught up in all that. She was beaten and left on the streets. After the riots, people came out into the streets to see the damage and carnage. Someone brought my sister to the local negro hospital. There were a lot of folks hurting so she didn't get the care she needed soon enough. By the time we were able to bring her home, she was just a shell of herself. Sometimes I wonder if it would have been better for her to just have died in those streets than to live the life it left her." She paused for a moment, as I took in all she had told me. My heart ached for what her sister and the others had been through.

"I hated white people for the longest time after that. Everyone I saw, I thought to myself, "Could you be one of those people who beat my sister?" I didn't trust them. I even hated Momma and Daddy for a spell. How could they not know that Mabel would try to sneak out and be a part of the protest? They heard how she'd say that something had to be done. We needed to stand up for ourselves. We needed to take back our dignity. They should have *known* what she'd do. Every time they'd try to talk to me about the attack, I'd just get up and leave the room. I only associated with them for mealtime and church.

"Momma had to quit her job to take care of her. Mabel needed full-time care. Daddy picked up extra hours when he could to help make ends meet, but it never seemed like it was enough. By the time I was old enough to start school, I knew I wanted to be a nurse like Mabel. I was taking care of her at this point. I would hum to her, and she'd smile. Sometimes, I would just sit with her. She couldn't talk anymore. So, I'd do the talking for us both. I'd tell her about my day at school or show her the turkey I made by tracing my opened hand. Sometimes, I'd ask her to help me with a math problem not because she could help, but because I thought if I'd ask her, she'd feel important.

"Just as I was starting nursing school, Mabel started declining. I did all that I could do to help my momma with her. Anytime I learned something new that I thought would help her, I'd rush home to try it. Nothing seemed to help. The day she died, I was holding her hand, humming "Because He Lives." She slipped away so peacefully, and I knew from that moment on, I wanted to be there as a comfort for those whose time was nearing the end. So, I became a hospice nurse.

"My first patient was an elderly, white man named Charles. He had stage four pancreatic cancer. By the time I was called in as his hospice nurse, he only had two weeks to live, or so the doctors said. He was on so much morphine, he just laid in his bed all day long. I had to change his under pads, bathe him, and keep his IVs going with medication. He had put in his living will that he didn't want any nutritional supplements to keep him alive. So, I watched him starve to death. Each day, his breathing was more labored. He just laid there with his mouth open; the air somehow finding its way into his lungs. As I tended to Mr. Charles, many thoughts crossed my mind. I could end his life at any moment, and no one would be the wiser. I could torture him, and he couldn't call out in pain or even tell anyone what I was doing to him. I had so much power over this man. I was the master, and he was the slave.

"As these thoughts raced through my mind the first few days of aiding Mr. Charles, I kept thinking about Mabel. How she had depended on me to take care of her. I made sure I kept up with her medication, her feeding tube, and her cleanings. She had to trust that I would do all that for her. Mr. Charles was in the same situation. He needed me. It didn't matter what color his skin was, he needed my care. He needed me to stand by my nurse's oath and take care of him. He needed me to give him comfort in his last days on this Earth. And that's what I did. Mr. Charles died within a week of my starting his care. Since him, I've had ten other patients that I've helped transition to the next life. I'd like to think Mabel would be proud of me."

I sat there for a moment letting all that Caroline had just told me to sink in. I started crying when she told me of the mounted policemen galloping into the crowds. I could picture the entire scene in my head and feel the horror of those people running for their lives.

I turned to face Caroline, with tears on my cheeks. "You must hate us." It was a simple sentence, but it carried so much meaning.

"No, Miss Edna, er, Edna. I don't hate you. I don't hate white folk. I don't hate Asian folk. I don't hate Jewish or Muslim folk. After taking care of Mr. Charles, I came to know that I don't hate people. I sometimes hate their actions. Hate their harsh words. But I don't hate people. I realized a long time ago that people are products of their upbringing. All races think, believe, and act because of the way they were brought up. The way their parents spoke and acted. The way their grandparents spoke and acted. Sometimes, though, the circle of hate and bigotry stops with them. They don't behave or believe as their parents or grandparents did. They see people as people. They know we all bleed red; we all have similar wants for our kids and our planet. They feel the pain of loss just like everyone else. They feel joy just like everyone else, too. They've broken the cycle. They want a better place for everyone. They may see different skin colors but it's only a description, not a distinction. Those people are whom I focus on. Those people: black, white, and brown, are going to change the world for the better.

"And I see you, Edna. You are one of those people. When you first saw me, you weren't thinking I was going to steal your silverware. You saw me as someone that was here to take care of you and to help you through the time you have left."

"Thank you, Caroline. Thank you for seeing that in me because that's exactly what I see in you. It hurts my heart so much to hear about all this generational hate. I've tried my best to be one of those cycle-breakers. To be honest, it wasn't much of a cycle to break. My family just sees people, neighbors, and friends. I'll be the first to start a conversation in an elevator. I'll hold the door for the person behind me. I've helped in shelters feeding the poor, and I've sponsored underprivileged children. Not out of any obligation, it's just the right thing to do. It's the human thing to do. I'm not looking for gold stars because I honestly believe we're all here for a reason and one of those reasons is to help one another," I humbly said.

Caroline and I just sat there for a few more minutes. I turned to her to ask, "What are you making?"

"Oh, this?" She inquired holding up her pale blue project. She had been crocheting the entire time she told me her story, never skipping a stitch. "It's going to be a baby blanket. My daughter, Mabel is having her first child, a boy, right around Christmastime," she said.

"You named your daughter after your sister?" I asked.

"Yes. When she was born, the doctors gave her to me once they weighed her and checked all her vitals. When they placed her in my arms, her eyes were open. I looked into those eyes, and I saw Mabel staring back at me. I knew right there and then that I had to name her after my sister. She's thirty now, and this is my first grandchild.

She waited until she and her husband finished their residency. They're both doctors. Her husband is a podiatrist, and she specializes in children with speech impediments." She beamed with pride.

"You must be so proud of them," I said.

"Yes, ma'am, I am. Oh, would you look at the time? It's almost time for Jonathan to start. Would you like me to fix you something to eat?" She said, starting to get up from the couch.

I patted her shoulder. "No, no. I'm fine. Truly. I think I'm going to try and get some more sleep. Thank you so kindly for telling me your story, Caroline. What a lovely legacy you will leave in this world. And I am truly sorry for the loss of your sister. I know you loved her very much, and you show her the love you had, and still have, for her with your love and caring for others. Goodnight, Caroline." I said as I got up from the couch and headed back toward my room.

DAY FOURTEEN

I slept the rest of the morning and late into the afternoon after staying up late talking with Caroline. By the time I got myself out of bed and dressed it was well after 5:00 PM. I heard Jonathan in the kitchen, so I walked in to see what he was doing.

"Good evening, Ms. Edna." He said as he turned from his task at the stove. I smelled a mixture of Mexican spices coming from the pans on the stove.

"What are you making, Jonathan?" I asked sniffing the air.

"Oh, just a little something I'm putting together. It's lean chicken with diced tomatoes, green peppers, and shallots. I've added some cumin and a dash of chili powder. It should be ready in a few minutes."

"That sounds delicious. Here, let me help you by setting the table while you finish up," I volunteered.

Once I had finished getting the plates and silverware placed on the table, Jonathan brought the meal over. At first taste, I closed my eyes and savored every flavor.

The chicken practically melted in my mouth as if he prepared it, especially for my limited capability to swallow food.

Another symptom of the cancer. Well, it doesn't matter right now, this shit is good!

"Mmm, this is good," I said with my mouth full of food.

"Thank you, Ms. Edna," he said sheepishly. "I like to experiment with food. I know it's hard for patients to eat, so I do my best to try to cut the pieces small enough for them but not too small that they burn while I'm cooking them."

"Did you go to culinary school or something before this job?" I inquired.

"Yes, ma'am. I did," he acknowledged. "I've always wanted to be a chef. I used to cook with my grandma on Sundays. She taught me how to cook the basics and then would sometimes allow me to add some finesse to the meal. She always supported my choices."

"How did you end up being a nurse, then?" I asked.

"Well, it's kind of funny how that all came about." He said grinning. "I finished high school with a plan. I was going to be an accountant. I know, how do you go from an accountant to a cooking nurse, right?" I nodded my head, shoveling the food into my mouth as he continued. "I was sitting in a boring finance class one day. The professor was droning on about profit and loss sheets, and budgeting. I really wasn't paying attention, so I started surfing the internet. I found this video of a cooking show and at the end of it, there was a contest. You had to submit a recipe and if you won, you won an entire line of cookware. I figured, what the hell, I'll enter. So, I did. The contest didn't end for another two months, and I honestly forgot that I entered. My grandma got sick about a week after I entered the contest, and my mom needed help taking care of her."

I'm sensing a theme here with these caretakers.

"I wasn't sure how I could help, but eventually, I got the hang of it and thought that I enjoyed making my grandma comfortable. I had put my college on pause while I was helping my mom, so when I went back after she passed, which was unfortunately rather quickly, I changed my major to nursing." He continued.

"I got the notice about a week later saying that I had won the contest! I was so excited, as you can imagine. After classes, I would come home and just start cooking recipes I found on the internet. And the rest is history. I decided to incorporate my love of cooking with my nursing career."

"Wow!" I said. "That's amazing that you were able to combine both your passions. But what made you become a hospice nurse?" I asked.

"To be honest, most of my patients are older. Older than you, that is. They remind me of my grandma. I saw how I could comfort her in her last days. You'd be surprised how many of my patients don't have family that takes care of them, and they just leave them in nursing homes; never visiting, and never checking in on them. Just leaving them there to die. I thought about taking a job at one of those homes, but I didn't think I could give the one-on-one care that I enjoy giving. So, I took a hospice job. One patient at a time that I can give my full attention to," he said.

"Your grandma would be proud of you, Jonathan," I said with tears welling up in my eyes. "Thank you for this delicious meal and thank you for sharing your story with me."

"It's been my pleasure, Ms. Edna," I didn't correct him to call me just Edna. He was still a kid in my eyes, so I let it pass and took a little bit of pleasure in the respect he showed.

DAY FIFTEEN

The day started as any day I had had recently. I woke up, rolled over, and looked at the clock. I'd be appalled that it was either too early or too late in the day. Stared at the ceiling for a bit, amazed that I even opened my eyes. The typical "check how you're feeling internally" type of day. I rolled out of bed and got dressed. I put on a pair of beige shorts and a white short-sleeve top with little red flowers on it. I slipped on some beige canvas shoes to match.

You look like an old lady. I am an old lady. Well, you don't have to look like one. Why don't you put on some short shorts and a halter top? Okay, for several reasons. One, I don't own short shorts, and two, no one owns halter tops. This isn't the 70s. Fair point... old lady.

As I walked into the living room to say good morning to Judy, I passed the calendar hanging by magnetic clips on the refrigerator. The month of July stared back at me. It was one of those calendars you get in the mail around September or October with kittens or puppies or some type of charitable organization's fundraiser pictures. They send them to you in hopes you will donate because you just love their calendar. I usually kept the calendar that had the cutest animals, threw away the rest, and threw away the "please send your donation to – in this self-addressed envelope – that we really would like you to use a stamp to save our costs" slip. July's picture was a pair of orange tabby kittens huddled together and looking directly at the camera, wild-eyed and oozing cuteness.

I noticed the date. It was July 15th. I stared at the black number as if it were coming off the shiny white block. I couldn't move. The realization of the day was sinking in, and I did not like the feeling. I started breathing hard as if I was just starting that burning, out-of-breath feeling you get when you haven't exercised in months and now you've decided to take up jogging. I stumbled into the living room. Judy was startled and asked me what was wrong as she started walking toward me. I brushed her off.

"I'm fine. I'm going for a walk," I told her as I bolted out the front door.

The day was on the cooler side for July. My mind instantly went to the dream I had a few nights before.

You're awake, idiot. Where are you going? I don't know. I needed to get out of that house. I can't breathe.

I didn't stop walking. I walked to the end of my street and turned right to stay on the sidewalk. Thoughts raced through my head. The whole concept of actually dying was weighing on me.

I don't want to die! Too late for that. No, it's not. This isn't fair. I want to live! I'm going to start exercising. I'm going to call the doctor today and get into that experimental treatment. I'm going to fight this! I have too much to live for. This is so fucking unfair. I'm mad! I don't want this! Please, God, stop this! Stop all of it. You can do it. I've been a good person. Why don't you just make this all go away?

I stopped and looked towards Heaven.

"Make it stop!" I shouted. I was breathing so hard that I had to stop to rest. As I started to catch my breath, I made up my mind: I'm going to live.

Still shaking from my excursion, I made my way back home.

I walked through the door, and I saw Judy's face pale. She rushed over to me and sat me on the couch. "What were you doing, running?"

"No. I want to live. I've decided I'm going to call Dr. Linder back and start the experimental treatment."

"Edna." She said softly placing her hand on my shoulder. "It's too late. The treatment would only *maybe* have given you more time if you had started it two weeks ago. As Dr. Linder said, it's a very aggressive cancer. I'm so sorry. It just won't work."

"Fuck you, Judy," I said standing up and stomping into my room. I flung myself down on the bed, still fuming from what Judy had said.

How dare she tell me it's too late! What does she know? I don't want to die, damn it! Well, I hate to tell you this sweetheart, but it's gonna happen. Like she said, it's too far gone. You'd just be making yourself sick and who wants that in the last days of their life? Shut up! You're not helping. What if the experimental crap worked and I was miraculously cured? Huh? Ever think of that, Sherlock? Ain't gonna happen, toots.

I laid there a few more minutes before I realized just how harsh I was with Judy. It wasn't her fault I decided in the eleventh hour to change my mind and fight to live.

You should apologize. I know. I will. Well, do it now. Okay, okay.

I sat up with my feet hanging over the bed, took a deep breath, and got up to go apologize to Judy.

DAY SIXTEEN

After having to eat crow yesterday for blowing up at Judy, I decided to get up, get dressed and put on my happy face to meet the day.

Judy was in the kitchen fixing breakfast. "Good morning, Judy," I said with the most pleasant voice I could muster. I even added, "You look nice, today" for good measure.

Judy accepted my apology yesterday, but I could tell that she was still pretty sore with me today. "Thank you, Edna." It was all she said.

We ate breakfast in silence for about five minutes, and then the phone rang. Judy got up from the table to answer the phone. "Yes, hold on, please," she said bringing the phone into the dining room. "It's Russell" was all she said as she handed me the phone.

I took the phone in my hands and just held it there. I hadn't called Russell. I knew the kids had told him the news, but he hadn't heard it from me yet. What could I say to him?

Hey, I know two weeks have passed and I haven't called... I've been busy dying. No, Idiot, that is not what you say.

"Hey, Russell. How are you?" was all I could come up with to start the conversation.

"Hi, Edna. Look. I'm not going to beat around the bush. Why didn't you tell me you were sick? How come I had to hear it from our hysterical kids? Do you know what it's like trying to calm Amelia down when she gets like that?" He blasted out the questions like an automatic weapon, and the bullets hit my heart directly.

"I'm sorry, Russell. I know I should have called you right after I talked to the kids. I could give you a thousand excuses for why I didn't, but I won't. Just please accept my apology," I said deflated.

"Do you mind if I come over for a bit?" He asked, cutting me off.

"Not at all. You know where I live," I said tensely.

Great, another confrontation. Maybe not, he did sound concerned. He's mad. How about, he's hurt? Yeah, maybe.

Judy answered the door when Russell knocked and showed him into my room. I was just sitting on the bed thinking about all the things I could say to him as to why I didn't tell him sooner.

I got nothing. Me either.

Russell sat down next to me and let out a sigh. "I'm sorry I snapped at you, Edna. I was hurt when I had to hear the news from the kids." *Told ya.* "I just wasn't prepared to handle Amelia when she called me so upset." He continued. "How are you feeling? Does it hurt?" he asked softly.

"Not really. I need morphine occasionally, mainly to help me sleep." I lied.

Russell put his arm around me and pulled me towards him. He kissed the top of my head as he said, "I'm so sorry, Edna. I wish there was something I could do for you."

With his arms around me and his lips on my head, I felt a familiar twinge. It was that familiarity you feel when you feel comforted. I leaned into Russell a little more. He lowered his head and softly kissed my cheek. I lifted my head and looked into his clear blue eyes. He lowered his head more and kissed my lips. I kissed him back. My body was tingling with urges deep in my soul. Still kissing him, I stood up and gently pushed myself into him, so he laid back on the bed.

He smelled like sandalwood cologne, and I drank it all in. We were like when we were married. The kissing became more intense. I pulled away staring down at him. "Are you sure about this?" I asked hoarsely. "Yes," was all he managed to say.

We made love like lovers who had been parted for a year. It had been many years since we made love, but it was like it was yesterday. I'm sure Judy figured out what was going on because I faintly heard the front door open and close. I didn't care. I felt urges that had long been dormant. We moved in a rhythm that we both knew the other needed. Each one of us triggering those desires.

Afterward, I rolled off Russell and laid my head on his chest. The bed was a standard hospital bed, so the accommodations for two people were narrow. It made me able to get very close to him. He wrapped his arms around me and stroked my hair with his hand. I felt so much peace, I didn't want it to end.

Why did you divorce him, again? I asked myself. *Shut up. It doesn't matter right now.*

I listened to the sound of his heartbeat. It was a strong heart, and the thought occurred to me that this heart would continue to beat long after I'm gone. At this moment, it didn't matter. The consistent thumping lulled me to sleep. I remember saying "I needed that" as I drifted off to sleep without any manufactured aid.

DAY SEVENTEEN

Sleep is so overrated. It was 7:30 AM, and I was wide awake. I don't know what woke me up or whether I just was so tired from yesterday. The lovemaking Russell and I did yesterday must have worn me out. I didn't hear him leave yesterday, and I must have slept through the entire day.

I don't have much time left, why am I sleeping? Um, because your body is wearing down. You don't have enough energy. You're weak. What other reasons do you want? Enough! Let's get this day started.

I got out of bed and got dressed. Caroline was leaving, and Judy was coming in. As I opened my bedroom door, I heard them whispering to one another. I couldn't make out all the words, but I did hear "ex-husband" and "I had to leave." I chuckled to myself at Judy's embarrassment.

I waited until I heard the door close before I entered the kitchen. Judy came in from the living room. Her cheeks turned blood red when she saw me and she stammered, "Good morning, Edna."

"It *is* a good morning, isn't it, Judy?" I couldn't help just rubbing in the awkwardness of the situation for her.

"Would you like me to fix you some breakfast?" she asked, clearing her throat, and trying to change the subject.

"Sure. Why don't you whip up something delicious?" I said with a grin. "I'm going to call Delores while you're doing that."

"Okay," she said, thankful for the distraction and the fact that I left the room.

"Delores, my friend!" I cheerfully said into the phone. "Why don't you come over today? Let's get into something."

"Sure. What are you thinking about doing?" she asked. I could tell she was taken aback by my overly joyful tone.

"Oh, I don't know. Hey! I do have an idea. Why don't we go horseback riding? The horse farm is only a couple of minutes away. Maybe we'll grab some lunch while we're out, too."

"Horseback riding, Edna? You want to go horseback riding? Like, getting on a horse and riding?" I could tell she was somewhat in shock.

"Yes, Delores. I want to mount a horse and ride it until it's breathless!" I said laughing.

"What are you smoking, Edna?" she asked.

"Nothing, but want to?" I said mischievously.

"Dear God, Woman. What is with you today? I'm coming over." She hung up the phone.

It didn't take long before Delores was rushing through my front door as if she was trying to see if I was in some sort of frantic state of mind. She abruptly stopped when she saw me calmly eating my breakfast.

"Good morning, bestie. How are you today? Ready for some adventure?" I asked as I chewed on the pancakes Judy had fixed for breakfast.

"You're serious, aren't you?" Delores asked, still befuddled by my sudden burst of energy.

"Yes, Delores. I am serious. I want to go horseback riding. I'm trying to make the most of everything I have left of my time. I don't want to fritter away these next few weeks lying in my bed drooling because I have had extra doses of morphine."

We headed over to the horse farm. 'Good Time Riding' was the name of the place. It had been around for about thirty years. The farm had started off as a small operation with three horses that belonged to the farm's owner, Emmet Charles. Mr. Charles had bought three horses for his children at the time to teach them to ride, dress, and take care of the animals. I think he thought that he'd have an award-winning equestrian farm with showcase thoroughbreds fit for the Kentucky Derby. Over time, he realized that he didn't have the funds to support that fantasy and just let the horses be rented out for a few hours a day for the pleasure of the community.

When we pulled up to the stalls, Mr. Charles III came out to greet us. "Good morning, ladies. What brings you to Good Time Riding today?"

"She wants to go horseback riding," Delores snickered. "Personally, I think she's out of her mind. She's in no condition to be riding a horse. Look at her, she's wasting away," she added.

"Shut up, Delores." I fired back. "Mr. Charles," I continued after giving Delores a sideways sneer, "My friend is somewhat correct. I probably shouldn't be riding a horse, but you see, I don't have very much time in my life, and I'd like to feel some kind of joy. I used to bring my kids here when your father ran the business. They had so much fun, and I'd like to feel a little bit of that now."

Mr. Charles III wasn't sure what to make of Delores and my comments, but he took it all in and simply said, "I think I have exactly what you need." He turned and walked away towards the horse stalls.

I swung around to Delores. "You need to be more supportive. I need this today and you need to be here for me."

"I'm sorry, Edna. You're right," Delores said with a sigh in her voice. "I just think this will be too much for you, that's all."

"It may be, but I don't want to just sit around waiting for death. I'm sick of being sick."

Mr. Charles III returned with two beautiful mares. One was a white horse speckled with reddish-brown markings. Her mane was reddish brown as well. She walked straight up to me as if she knew what was happening in my body and just nuzzled her face into my shoulders. I felt an instant connection.

"What's her name?" I asked.

"Oh, that's Rosy. She's our gentlest mare," Mr. Charles III said. "She seems to have taken a liking to you."

"Yes, she has," I said, rubbing her long face. Rosy softly snorted.

The other mare was a beautiful, shimmering grey horse. She whinnied a little as she approached Delores. Delores seemed a little nervous and the horse sensed it.

"I haven't ridden a horse before," she stated as her voice cracked.

"Oh, Lizzy is a good mare!" Mr. Charles III assured Delores. "You won't have any problems with her."

Delores and I mounted our horses. Mr. Charles III showed us the paths we would be taking and sent us off. When we were a few hundred yards from the stables, I nudged Rosy a little and her trot increased in speed. I felt the exhilaration of the horse, my surroundings, the wind in my hair, and the pure joy of the adventure. I urged Rosy a little faster. My heart started pounding as we crossed the open meadow. I loved the speed and wanted more.

"Faster, girl," I whispered in Rosy's ear. She sped up a little more. Soon we were at full speed. It was as if Rosy knew exactly what I needed. The meadow was a blur as we raced ahead. My hair was blowing behind me; the wind was warm on my face as it whistled by.

Suddenly, Rosy started slowing down. My breath was caught in my chest. I couldn't gasp enough air. My chest started tightening. Panic set in. Rosy must have sensed my trauma and slowed even more to a walking pace. I grabbed my chest, struggling to catch my breath. I heard Delores in the background screaming my name. I was gasping for air by the time she caught up to us.

"Edna!" She shouted. "Edna, are you okay?" She looked at me in horror. Her eyes were wide and frantic.

"Can't breathe." It was all I could say. The horses stopped, and I just sat still on Rosy trying to breathe. Ever so slowly, the calmness of Rosy helped calm me down and my breathing returned to normal. It felt as if an hour had passed before I was able to breathe normally, albeit still labored.

Deflated, I turned to Delores with tears in my eyes, "You were right, Delores. This wasn't such a good idea. Let's go home." I turned Rosy back towards the stables before Delores could say a single word.

Delores and I were silent on the short ride home. When we pulled into the driveway, I turned to Delores. The peppiness I had had before we left for the farm was gone.

"I'm sorry for today, Delores. I don't know what I was thinking. I had felt so alive this morning as if nothing was wrong with me. I just wanted that feeling to continue. I wanted to feel good again. I wanted to not think about how the cancer was ravishing my body. Today I felt as if it was gone. I felt normal." All the energy I felt earlier today was no longer evident in my voice.

"I'm sorry, Edna. I really am. But you can't go on like this. It's not going away, and it seems it's time for other treatments." Delores said matter-of-factly. She could be firm when she needed to be, and this was one of those times. "I think we need to talk to Judy about what happened and get her opinion on what should be done next." Delores was right, I just didn't want to admit it. Mainly, I didn't want to admit it to Judy.

DAY EIGHTEEN

T-minus twelve days and counting.

Really? This is how you're going to start the mornings from now on. What else have I got to do?

I rolled over to get out of bed, and I noticed something in my nose. I reached my hand up and felt plastic tubing.

What the hell is this? It's your oxygen, silly. Don't you remember that little "gasping for air" episode you had yesterday? Well, you got yourself into a pickle, and this is the result. Air. Now you don't have to gasp for it, just turn up the dial.

Shit!

I also noticed the Do Not Resuscitate notice hanging on my wall.

Where did that come from? They put it in when they brought the bed and all the other equipment. You signed the papers; it's required to be posted. I'm surprised you haven't noticed it yet. Maybe I wanted to ignore it. Did you ever think of that?

Maybe I just want to bury my head in the sand until it's all over.

This is all too real! What did you expect? I don't know. Maybe to not see, I mean really see, all the preparations going on around me surrounding my impending death.

Sorry, sweetheart, that's the way the cookie crumbles.

I rolled back over and stayed in bed the rest of the day, snorting air from the tubes in my nose.

DAY NINETEEN

I sat in the living room with Judy, reading my newspaper. I wish I could put my finger on what I didn't like about her. She was so professional, for lack of a better word. It was as if she was a humanized robot. She did her job, showed hardly any emotion, and came and went precisely at her appointed times. No more, no less.

I kept glancing over at her as I pretended to read. She was sitting straight, no slouching for Judy. She was reading a book that seemed to be about hummingbirds. At least, there was a hummingbird on the cover, so that's what I assumed. I looked at her crisp white nursing shoes. The ones with the inch and a-half sole, white laces, and white leather material. She was wearing light blue capri pants that appeared to be made from linen. She wore a loose, but not overly loose, pale-yellow blouse along with a thin, tan sweater. I would guess her to be around 65 years old. Probably too old to be taking care of people, but I hadn't bothered to ask her story.

Maybe you should change that.

"Judy?" I started. Just as she turned to me, my mother came through the door. I hadn't heard her car pull into the driveway. Probably because I was intently reviewing Judy's wardrobe.

"Mom," I said as I started to get up to greet her. "What brings you over?" I queried.

"Oh, I was just driving around and thought I'd stop by." She said. "What is that in your nose?" She asked as she noticed the oxygen tubing.

"Umm, it's just some oxygen, Mom. Nothing to worry about." I tried to sound positive as I watched the pity form on her face. It was hopeless to try and fool my mother. The reality of the situation set in, and now she was furrowing her brow and wringing her hands.

"Edna," She said sternly, "It is something to worry about. Why are you on oxygen now?" She leaned in close enough that I could feel her breath mixing with pure oxygen swirling in my nose.

There are times that I just want to grab my mother by the shoulders, look her dead in the eyes and say, *"Why do you think, Captain Obvious?"* However, I took a deep breath through my mouth and slowly let it out, and said, "The doctor felt it was necessary given the deteriorating condition of my lungs, Mom."

That'll shut her up. Way to go, Edna. Look at her face collapsing.

"Come into the kitchen, Mom. Let me get you something to drink. Judy just made some sweet tea this morning. Why don't you have a glass?" I said as I ushered her into the kitchen, my arms around her shoulders.

The tubing caught onto something, and I stumbled.

What the hell?

"Mom! Watch where you're walking. You just stepped on my tubing." I said, exasperatedly.

"Oh, my! I'm so sorry, Edna. I'm so sorry," she cried.

"It's okay, Mom. Why don't you sit down?" I guided her to the table and away from my tubing.

I sat Mom down and poured her a glass of tea. I watched as she took a sip, savoring the flavor. I will admit, Judy did make some good southern sweet tea. "That's good," she said, setting her glass on the table.

Before she could start her pity party on me, I interjected, "What did you want to talk to me about, Mom?" I said heading up the conversation.

"Are you still going through with this party? I mean, seriously Edna, look at you. You're so thin, and now you have to drag around an oxygen tank. Someone could step on the tubing and cut off your supply. Don't you think you're doing too much?" she asked irately. "And I heard you went horseback riding yesterday. What were you thinking? You could have fallen off the horse and broken your neck. Where would that have landed you? In the hospital!" Her voice sounded like the chiding mother she could be at times.

"Mom," I said as gently as I could through gritted teeth. My mother had a way of speaking that sounded like she was chiding me for being stupid or unreal. The tone of her voice sometimes felt like nails on a chalkboard; screeching slowing down, sinking that sound into your very soul. It took me back in time to when I was sixteen years old.

I had been out with some friends whom my mother thought were not the best influence on me. What teenage kids are a good influence? We had decided to harmlessly toilet paper a house in the neighborhood. The problem was we decided to do it at two o'clock in the morning. We had almost finished the job when the owner of the house, unbeknownst to us worked a 6 PM to 2 AM job, came home, and caught us. There was a lot of yelling, and we scrambled. Unfortunately, he recognized me because his wife and my mother were both on the PTA.

So, the next morning, my mother dragged me out of bed at 8 AM and let me have it. Talking about how irresponsible I was. How my friends were good-for-nothing hoodlums that would end up in jail. How embarrassed she was that she would have to face the wife at the next meeting. How disappointed in me she was. This went on and on for about an hour before she laid down the punishment. I wasn't allowed to see my friends that entire summer, and I spent my days mowing the lawn, painting the fence, and sweeping the porch of the house I had toilet-papered. I wasn't a very happy sixteen-year-old, and I blamed it all on my mom. And now, I felt as if I were that teenager all over again, but this time she wasn't going to intimidate me.

"We've been over this. I want to say goodbye while I can. How many funerals have you attended just to say goodbye to someone? Well, guess what? They don't know you're there. A funeral is for the living. The dead don't care. However, I do care," I said impatiently. "I want to be here to say goodbye, to hear the goodbyes. I want to hug people and let them know I'll be okay. I want to tell them to carry on, not dwell on the sadness. Basically, I want people to know it's okay to let go while I can. I don't know how much longer I will have the strength to do so. I don't know how much longer I have until the morphine becomes a permanent drip in my arm. I don't know how much longer I'll be aware my family is even in the room with me, let alone be able to have a conversation with them. This is real, Mom. It isn't going away. I'm not scheduled for some Divine intervention. No miracles for me, Mom," I tried to make her see that this was important to me. It was something I needed to do. Too many times I had attended funerals just to see family and friends say that they had wished they had spent more time with the deceased or should have stopped by months before they passed just to catch up on small talk.

My mother just sat there, no words to be found. I tried to put myself in her shoes. I tried to feel what she was feeling, but I just couldn't. I was being selfish, I know. I should be comforting her, letting her know it was okay. Wasn't that just what I had been telling her I wanted to do? I just couldn't. I wanted to feel sorry for myself. I wanted to feel depressed. Just for a moment, I didn't want to be strong.

And then, I couldn't do it anymore. My annoyingly selfless nature kicked in. I got up and went to my mother and hugged her. My body was wracked with sobs along with hers. She was going to have to bury her daughter. No mother should have to bury their child. I was putting myself in her shoes now, and she needed comfort. We sat there hugging and crying for a few more minutes before I pulled away.

"Come on, Mom. Let's focus on something else for a bit," I said, trying to change the subject. "I was wondering if you could come over tomorrow around noon and bring some lunch for you, me, and Amelia. She's going to be decorating the place for the party, and I'm sure she could use some help."

"I'd be glad to help, Edna. You're right. We need to change focus. I can be sad, but I can also be here for you as you need me. I don't want to smother you, but I do want you to know that I am here. The biggest part of me wants to spend as much time as I can while you're still here, but I also know that you need your space. It's a very difficult line to walk; please understand that, Sweetie."

"I know, Mom and I really appreciate you saying that," I said, trying my best to give her something in my voice that reflected I welcomed her need to be understood.

DAY TWENTY

T-minus TEN.

Would you stop? Oh, come on. How could I pass up TEN? I mean, that's the big one. That's the one that gets everyone's attention. Fine. You can have your ten, but will you stop now? Sure.

Amelia and Mom must have ridden together because they both showed up precisely at noon. Amelia brought some more party favors with her and carried them into the dining room. "I just saw these and I had to add them to the theme," she said holding up mini-Styrofoam tombstones.

"You found them?" I said, pleasantly surprised in a morbid sort of way.

"Yep. I guess when I went to the party store before they received their Halloween decorations. But now that it's after the Fourth, everyone has them in stock. I even saw some Christmas decorations here and there in the store." Her voice caught in her throat as soon as she said Christmas.

"That's awesome, Honey!" I quickly interjected before Amelia could get hung up on the thought of the approaching holiday without her mother. "They'll add to the theme – merry mortality," I said smiling, trying to make light of the situation.

I looked over at my mother. She wasn't happy with the whole "morbid" theme, but she didn't say anything. She just started pulling the plastic wrap off the various plates and cutlery.

Mom and Amelia started putting the decorations out. I just watched as the two generations tried to work out the thoughts in their heads about what they were actually doing. Amelia was hanging black streamers wherever she felt looked best, and mom was stacking paper plates, plastic cups, and cutlery in neat piles along the kitchen island.

I started to feel a little pain in my right leg, so I decided to sit down and watch. The pain started intensifying.

Probably from riding that damn horse yesterday.

I continued to make small talk with my mother and daughter. I asked Amelia about the guest list.

"Don't worry, Mom. I took care of all the invites," she said enthusiastically. "There were some people that just didn't want to come because of the idea. I guess they missed the point of what you were trying to do."

"So, how many people do we have coming?" I asked. The pain was becoming almost unbearable, but I had to keep the conversation going so as to not show what was happening in my body.

"I think there will be about 12 people. That's not too much for you, is it?" She asked with concern in her voice.

"No, honey. I think that should be fine," I answered.

Mom looked over at me and immediately asked, "What's wrong, Edna?"

I guess she could tell that I was fidgeting a little too much, and I'm sure she noticed the ever-so-slight change in my voice.

Mothers know you know.

"I'm just having a little pain today, that's all," I replied trying to lighten the tone in my voice. "I probably overdid it yesterday with my horseback riding adventure."

"I told you I didn't think it was a good idea," she said, proceeding to chide me to Amelia as if Amelia would listen to her.

They debated whether it had been a good idea or not, totally ignoring my presence.

The pain was becoming too unbearable. I wanted so badly to be able to sit there and enjoy the company of my mother and daughter.

Go away, pain. Just go away. It can't, Edna. It's spreading, and it won't stop. I KNOW THAT! Why don't you just tell them you need to go lay down? They can finish this up without you. I don't want to go lay down; I want the pain to go away!

"Hey, guys," I said, interrupting the debate of my foolishness that was going on between my two favorite people. "Do you mind if I leave the decorating to you? I think I need to lay down a bit."

My mother and daughter spoke at the same time. "Are you okay?"

"I'm just tired and in some pain at the moment," I said.

"Sure, Mom. Grandma and I can finish this up for you," Amelia said looking to my mother for affirmation.

"Of course, Sweetie. We can finish for you. Why don't you lay down, and we'll come to see you when it's all finished?" Mom added.

I got up from the chair, nodding to my mother and daughter. I walked into the living room where Judy was reading another magazine. "Judy, can you come with me into my room for a moment?"

"Of course," she said, closing the magazine.

"I think I need a dose of morphine," I said quietly as we entered my room. "I'm experiencing a lot of pain in my legs, and I'm not feeling too well."

"I can do that for you," she said, matter-of-factly.

I laid down on the bed, and Judy gave me my shot. I heard her leave the room, softly closing the door.

As I lay there feeling the morphine slowly relaxing me, I thought about what was going on inside my own body. Although I couldn't feel the cancer, per se, I imagined tiny, little cells gnawing away at my bones and organs, like termites eating away at old deck boards. Constantly chewing until it was all consumed.

I could barely hear Amelia and my mother talking about where to put decorations, where people were going to sit, hoping it wouldn't rain, and if they were sure that a party was the right thing to be having right now.

The morphine pull was getting stronger, and I couldn't fight the sleep that was taking over my body. I dosed off thinking about little gremlins with large, sharp teeth biting into my bones, fighting them off with what little immunity-armored white blood cells I had left. It was a battle I was losing.

DAY TWENTY-ONE

It was raining. I laid in bed thinking about tomorrow and hoping I would have the strength to have this party. Mom and Amelia had done a great job decorating. I knew my mom wasn't too keen on the whole idea of a party. I tried to make her understand that it was what I needed. I explained to her that seeing my friends and family before I died meant the world to me. I knew some of them would be uncomfortable and I put myself in their shoes.

You wouldn't go. Yes, I would. If Delores wanted a going away party, I'd go. Yeah, but would you go to Karen's? Probably not.

The rain was soothing. I could hear the different sounds of the raindrops hitting the windows. Sometimes it was heavy rain, other times it was soft.

I thought about the birds hiding in the trees waiting for it all to stop so they could start singing again; start searching for food again. It amazed me how the birds and other animals knew well before we did that a storm was coming. They knew the difference between a cloudy day and thunder clouds.

The rain continued well into the afternoon, and I just laid there. Judy came in now and again to ask how I was feeling or if she could get me anything. I politely said, "No."

I thought about the people I was going to say goodbye to tomorrow. *What would they say to me?* I hoped there wouldn't be too many tears. I wondered if they'd like the food. *Would they even be able to eat?* It was hard for me to eat when I was upset. Other people used food as a comfort when melancholy set in.

What are you going to wear tomorrow? The weatherman said it was going to be a perfect night.

A rare cold front had settled into the area, and the temperature and humidity were going to be low. I wondered if God knew that I needed this party and gave me perfect weather. People wouldn't be able to use the excuse that the weather wasn't good in order not to come. Not that they still wouldn't come, but people can be finicky like that.

Get Up! I have to pee.

DAY TWENTY-TWO

Wake up! It's party time! Whoop, whoop! Time to dance, drink and have a good time. Time to put the cancer to the left and let your right side take over! Get up! Okay, okay. I'm getting up! Geez!

I got out of bed, leaving the clothes on that I had on yesterday. *You should try to change into pajamas or something before you get a dose of your sleepy medicine. Do you think? I'm going to take a shower. Does it matter which clothes I take off? Good point.*

I dragged my oxygen tank along with me into the bathroom. I stood there for a moment trying to figure out how to get into the shower with the tubing attached to my face. I turned the water on while I thought about the best way to do this. I decided to take the nostril piece off, throw the hose over the shower rod, and stepped into the shower.

After adjusting the water temperature from a Hell-heated stream to a bearable degree, I looped the hose over my ears and stuck the nose piece in my nostrils. I stood there letting the warm water cascade over my body, savoring the feel of it. Water flowed down my face, and I accidentally breathed in through my nostrils causing the water to be inhaled. After a few moments of coughing, I finally caught my breath again and finished the shower, mindful of the water.

Showering and drying off took a lot of my energy so, I sat down on the toilet seat as I recovered.

Damn! The simplest things are taking their toll on me. Get used to it, toots. It's only going to get worse.

I made my way back to my bedroom and got dressed. It was 3 o'clock in the afternoon. The guests would be here in just a couple of hours.

God, please let me have the strength to get through this night without having any severe incidents, I prayed. *Just take it slowly, sit a lot, and don't drink. What's the fun in that? It's up to you, but I wouldn't. You're probably right.*

After I finished getting dressed, I went into the living room to talk to Judy.

"Judy, as you know, I'm having a party today. Whether you agree with it is immaterial. What I want from you is something to ease any pain I might start to have, but something that isn't strong enough to knock me out," I stated.

"Do you want me to give you some Oxycontin now or do you want to wait to take something until closer to the party? If you want me to leave instructions with Jonathan to give you something when he comes in at 4, I can do that," she asserted.

"Oh, yeah, that makes sense. I don't want to take anything now. If I need it, I'll ask Jonathan. Thank you," I said. "I forgot that you are getting ready to leave. I'll save you some cake," I said, trying to be nice.

"Oh, no thank you, Edna. I need to watch my sugar. I'm getting a little heavier than I'd like," she replied.

Rub it in, why don't you? Smile. Just smile. *No smart-ass reply is needed. Except maybe I should point out how heavy she really is. No, don't.*

Jonathan came in a few minutes afterward, and Judy left him with the instructions she and I had spoken about.

"So, tonight's the big party, huh? Is there anything I can help with? You are familiar with my cooking skills, yes?" Jonathan asked, emphasizing his culinary expertise with a grin.

"Not this time, Jonathan. It's all being catered by Pete's. In fact, they should be here in about an hour to set up. Would you mind helping with that?" I solicited.

"No problem. I'd love to. That's a great choice for a caterer. Their food is exceptional. I hope you ordered some of their honey barbecue pulled pork. That's stuff is off the hook good," he said like a kid in a candy store.

"Of course, I did! That's like one of their most famous items. Couldn't have them cater a party without it. Oh, and feel free to help yourself tonight. I don't want a lot of leftovers; maybe enough for you guys to have lunches or something during your shifts," I told him.

"Thanks!" he said. "Judy informed me that you may need some medication tonight, is that right?" he asked.

"Yeah, I've been in a lot of pain lately, and I don't want to ruin the party by being a zombie, so I asked her if you'd be able to give me something to take the edge off without me drooling in a puddle somewhere," I said.

"It's the cancer getting worse, you know," Jonathan said to me with a touch of sympathy in his voice. "I can give you the medication about half an hour before your guests start arriving. It may make you a little loopy, but, because it's targeting the pain, it shouldn't knock you totally out. When everyone leaves, I can then give you some morphine to eliminate any residual pain you may be experiencing and then you can sleep the rest of the night."

"Thank you, Jonathan," I replied taking a deep breath, trying to prepare myself for the evening.

Delores came over a little before six to make sure I was okay and to see if there were any last-minute preparations she could help with before everyone started arriving.

"You're looking good tonight, dear," she said to me as she came through the door. "Got a hot date or something?" she added, winking.

"You're funny," I said sounding a little muffled. *Oh yeah, that's the oxy drug right there. Keep it together.*

Amelia and Kevin drove together with Paula, Gracie, and Henry. "Don't worry, Mom," Amelia said when she saw the concerned look on my face as my grandchildren came through the door. "Stephanie is going to pick Gracie and Henry up and take them to my house for a sleepover. She'll be here in about 20 minutes. Kevin and I thought that you might want to see them real quick tonight."

"Wonderful!" I exclaimed. "Come here and give Grammy some kisses," I said as my two precious grandchildren ran into my arms. "Oh, how I love your hugs and kisses!"

Others started arriving. Karen and Ken from the bank. They weren't a couple, just coworkers. When I worked with them at the bank and had to call them over to show them how to make foreign deposits or exchange currency for vacationers traveling out of the country, I'd always think of that movie, "A Fish Called Wanda." In the scene where Kevin Kline's character, Otto, was stuck in the cement, and Ken was going to run him over with a steamroller. He kept saying, "Look! It's K-K-K-Ken, coming to k-k-k-kill me."

Russell came, and he brought a few of our mutual friends: Jake, Billy and Lisa, and Tom. Jake and I had flirted with each other some after Russell and I divorced. We went to dinner a few times and even tried kissing. Realizing that all of that just felt weird, like brother and sister weird, we decided just to remain friends. Jake would help me out with some of the house chores that I just wasn't able to do, like fixing a leaky faucet or power washing the siding. He'd stay occasionally, for dinner, but we always avoided any relationship conversations. I thought at one time he was serious about a girl he had been dating for almost a year, but she broke it off just before the one-year mark, and that was that.

Billy and Lisa had been married about five years when Russell and I met them. We were at some seafood fundraiser for Russell's work, and they were seated at our table. They had kids around the same ages as Kevin and Amelia, so we had that in common. Russell and Billy were into fishing, and that was the tie that bound them together. Lisa was a receptionist will little ambition. She and I didn't have a lot in common except for being moms. A few times over the years, we'd take a short vacation together. We'd all chip in to rent a house on the beach. We'd bring the kids, go swimming, cook hamburgers, and have hot dogs on the grill. Then we'd sit around and drink once the kids were in bed.

After Russell and I divorced, I didn't see Billy and Lisa as much. Billy was much more of a friend to Russell than Lisa was a friend to me. Not that we all didn't get along, it's just those things happen when there's a divorce. It's kind of like deciding who gets custody of the friends. Nobody is ever happy with the outcome.

Tom was a unique character. He was shy at first but, once you got to know him, you just couldn't shut him up. He read books a lot, seemed to know a little about a lot of different subjects, and he would let you know it too. Tom rented a house that Russell and I lived next to. We'd see him from time to time fixing the lawn mower or doing odd jobs around the house where he lived. He rented from a woman who had inherited the house from her grandparents. She had had no clue how to take care of it, so Tom was the perfect renter. She reduced his rent payments for the work he did on the house.

Eventually, she got tired of the paperwork and taxes on the house and sold it to Tom for a steal. He still lived in the house as far as I knew. At one time, I tried to fix Tom up with Delores. She thought he was cute and gave it a go. She soon found out that her extroverted personality and his introversions were no match. She could only take so much before she'd accuse him of stifling her. She was just too much of a free spirit.

My mother was the last to arrive. I knew how hard this must be on her. I could see it in her eyes. I also saw determination as she wasn't going to let her feelings get in the way of me having one last good time. I could see her swallowing any sorrowful comments she was about to say as she gave me a hug.

"Sorry I'm late, sweetie. Traffic was a bitch!" she said with good humor. I knew it took a lot for her to say that, and I was glad she kept it light.

The food arrived at 6:30 PM as promised, and everyone helped bring it into the kitchen. Pete delivered everything himself. I asked him to stay a bit, but he declined saying that he had to get home. It was his wife's birthday. He wanted to deliver the food himself, however, to make sure it was perfect, he told me.

"Thank you, Pete," I said giving him a hug.

"It's no problem, Ms. Edna. I hope you enjoy the food and your company. If there's anything missing, you call the store and let them know. They'll send someone over right away," he said.

I saw Amelia stop Pete before he went out the door. They both stepped outside together and then Amelia returned about five minutes later. I asked her what she talked to Pete about.

"Oh, I wanted to give him a tip for bringing the stuff over, and I also wanted to ask him something," she pulled on her lip with her teeth after she finished her sentence.

"What about?" I inquired.

"Um, I, uh, wanted to ask him, uh, if, uh he'd be able to, uh, provide food for your service," she quickly spoke that last part.

"Oh, that's a great idea. I hadn't thought about that," I told her, hugging her shoulders. Amelia seemed relieved.

We entered the kitchen together as everyone was filling their plates. I heard the comments about how great the food was and what great choices were from Pete's menu. The smells of the barbecue and cornbread filled the house.

I slowly made my way over to the island and grabbed a plate. "Here, Mom, let me get a plate for you," Kevin said, and he took the plate out of my hands. "Whatcha want to eat?"

"I'd really like some of that awesome barbecue before everyone eats it all! Give me some cornbread while you're at it. I'm starving," I cheerfully lied.

When everyone finished eating, we all went outside to watch the sunset. People were finishing conversations they started at the kitchen island. A few commented about how nice the weather was for July. I pulled my oxygen tank over to one of the chairs and sat down. My guests stopped their conversations to come over to see me. One by one, I spoke to them and told them how happy I was that they could make it tonight. After people walked away to start back up their conversations with one another, Paula came over and sat next to me.

"How are you holding up, Edna," she asked.

"To be honest, I'm a little tired," I said. "But I don't want you to say anything just yet. Let me enjoy the company a little while longer."

"No problem. I'll just sit here with you if you don't mind," she said putting her feet up on the chair. "Can I ask you something?" she asked after a few minutes.

"Of course, Paula."

"Does it hurt?" she blurted. "I mean, I'm sorry, I don't know why I said that." She sounded mortified.

"It's okay. Really. I don't mind. Yes, it does hurt. Each day it hurts more and more. That's why I wanted this party. Before the pain was too unbearable for me to even speak. I know it's coming. I know people are sad. Hell, I'm devastated, if you want the truth. This isn't how I wanted my last days to be. I wanted to be one of the lucky ones and just pass peacefully in my sleep. I guess it wasn't my fate."

"There's nothing, not even a little bit, that the doctors can do to stop this?" She asked, concerned.

"Nah, it's too far gone. It's my own damn fault for waiting too long to go to the doctor. Yeah, I should have gone two years ago. I guess maybe I thought it would go away on its own. Or I was imagining things. Or had that sense of immortality of, it would never happen to me." I said as I shook my head.

"Women need to start paying attention to their bodies more. Too often we get caught up in taking care of everyone else, and we push our own issues aside. We get so caught up with taking care of everyone else... husbands, kids, friends, and even parents. We think this ache or this pain is nothing; it'll go away. We'll take aspirin and try to forget it. We need to start listening and acting when those things come up. Usually, it isn't just a one-time thing either. It persists, yet we ignore it. Promise me, that if you start feeling anything out of sorts, you'll get it checked out. Please keep an eye on Amelia too. I know you two don't have the relationship she and Kevin do, but I'm asking you to keep watch over her if you can," I pleaded with Paula with sincerity.

"I will, Edna. I promise," she simply said. I knew I was asking a lot of Paula. She was going to be the glue that kept the family together. She was going to be the one to plan the birthday parties, the Thanksgiving dinner, and the Christmas get-togethers. I was asking her to basically take over my role. She knew it too. I could see it in her eyes.

While I finished speaking with Paula, I noticed Jonathan come outside and walk toward Kevin. As he was talking Kevin glanced my way and then shot his attention back to Jonathan as if he didn't want me to notice him looking my way. Jonathan then went over to where Delores and Jake were standing (a little too close for just casual) and started chatting with them before moving on. I smiled knowing Jake was taking his promise to me a little too seriously, but it made me happy.

Delores is going to get a grilling over this. You know she's going to leave with him. Good for her!

One by one, people came over to me telling me what a wonderful time they had, and that the food was great. Jonathan must have decided it was time for the party to be over.

Each grabbed my hand and patted it as if I were some long, lost, scared puppy. "Had a great time." "Talk to you soon." "Thanks for inviting me." Everyone basically saying their goodbyes.

It's what you wanted, remember? Yeah, but I didn't think it would end so soon.

Slowly, everyone said their goodbyes. I told Delores that I wanted to see her tomorrow. She had a sheepish look on her face knowing I knew what she was doing, or about to do, with Jake. I didn't care. Let her be happy for a night. Lord knew she needed it.

I started to clean up the kitchen and Jonathan stopped me. "I'll get all this. Why don't you lay down and I'll give you something stronger for the pain? I know you must be in some pain."

"I am. I thought I could go on a little longer tonight, but I just can't. Thank you."

Jonathan followed me into the room. He helped me change clothes and lay down on the bed. He administered the morphine, turned out the light, and quietly closed the door.

DAY TWENTY-THREE

The next day when I woke up, my body told me I had overdone it the night before. I just laid there thinking of the little gremlins again eating away at me. I took my mind off the internal feast going on by thinking about what everyone had said to me last night.

After I had gone outside and sat down, Jake was the first to come to talk with me. "Edna," he said, taking my hands, "You look marvelous." Jake kissed my cheek and sat down in the chair next to me.

"You're such a liar, Jake," I smiled.

"Okay then, you look like shit," he retorted.

"That's better," I giggled.

"I really appreciate Amelia reaching out to me and inviting me tonight. I know it's been a while since I've been around. I guess you never realize how time keeps flying by you, and how you never think of what's going on in other people's lives until you get news like this."

"It's okay, Jake. We all do that. If we thought about everybody every day, and what they're doing or what's going on in their lives, we'd never get anything done for ourselves. We are designed to be selfish that way."

Jake was taken aback when I said 'selfish.'

"Hey, Edna, I'm really sorry I haven't been in touch," he started.

"You misunderstand me, Jake," I explained. "I'm not blaming or condemning you in the least. It's just a matter of fact. I do it too. When's the last time I called you just to shoot the breeze or check to see how you are doing?" I asked.

"I see your point," he said slightly nodding in agreement. "So, how are you feeling? Is there anything I can do for you now?" he asked.

"Just coming to see me is enough, Sweetie," I told him. "I wanted a farewell party. I know it's a little on the morbid side, but how many times do we say goodbye to someone who's laying in a coffin? They don't know we're there. They can't hear us," I said.

"You can do one thing for me," I started. "I'd like you to keep up with Delores. This is hard on her, and she doesn't have many people to lean on. I'm not saying to nag her or anything, just check in with her occasionally. Don't just call. She'll just say everything is fine.

Stop by and see her. Look around to see if the house needs any repairs. You're good with that sort of stuff. If you see anything, just fix it because I know she'll say she'll get to it later."

"I'd be happy to do that for you, Edna, and for Delores," Jake glanced in Delores' direction. When he turned back to face me, he didn't finish his sentence. His face simply softened.

I noticed Karen and Ken were making their way over to me. Jake saw it too and finished up his conversation with me by leaning over and kissing my cheek again.

"Farewell, Edna, and Godspeed." He spoke. He touched his hand to his heart and left.

As they approached, Karen looked at Ken nervously. I knew they both felt somewhat awkward and were unsure of what to say.

"Hey, guys!" I said lightheartedly, trying to ease the mood. "How did you enjoy the barbecue?"

"Oh, it was great, Edna! I knew Pete's had good food, but I didn't know it was that good," Ken stated.

"Yes, it was wonderful. I know I ate too much!" Karen exclaimed.

"I want to thank you both for coming this evening. I know it's been some time since we last spoke or did anything together really. I guess what they say is true, that you are only family until some leaves the job." The words sounded harsh, and I didn't mean it that way. Trying to correct myself, I stuttered. "I mean, it's just that we all spent five days a week together for ten years, so we always had something to say or tell each other about our daily lives, and when you stop working together, sometimes that connection gets broken."

"I know what you mean, Edna," Karen interrupted. "And none of us wanted to see that happen. When you were there at the bank, we shared so many stories about our families. It all came naturally, talking about the kids and what crazy things they did, like when Kevin played soccer and kicked the referee in the groin by accident. Or when my daughter decided to take her underpants down in the hardware store when she saw a toilet on the sales floor.

I guess it's a natural state of things that goes away when someone leaves. I didn't mean to stay away or stop calling." She was getting upset with the conversation, and I needed to calm her down. *Karen was always a little overdramatic. Stop... she's nervous. Yeah, and feeling a little guilty I bet.*

"Please don't overthink things, Karen," I said sympathetically. "It happens to all of us. I'm just glad you and Ken decided to come. Our friendship, our work-family relationship, meant and still means a lot to me. You both were there when I needed you for life's ups and downs, and I'd like to think that I was there for you two as well," I stated gently.

"Oh yes, Edna. You were. The bank wasn't the same without you," Ken finally spoke up. "I would have never gotten through my breakup with Len without you," I chuckled at his mention of Len. Ken and Len. Len and Ken.

Billy and Lisa were headed my way now. Karen was relieved at the interruption. "You take care of yourself, Edna," she said before realizing the words she spoke. She abruptly turned away. In hindsight, it was a bad idea to invite her. Karen was never good at serious matters. Ken patted my hands and softly said "goodbye" before he put his arm around Karen's shoulder, escorting her away.

"Hey lady. How are you holding up?" Lisa asked.

"I'm hanging in there. I'm glad you two decided to come. I know it's been a few years since we got together. What's been happening with you guys?" I inquired.

"You know, typical stuff. Kids growing up. Grey hairs popping up here and there. Billy getting fat," Lisa laughed. Billy took the ribbing in stride and fired back "Lisa falling in love with her Botox doctor." Lisa gave him a soft punch in his side and sat down.

"In all seriousness, Edna. We're so sorry to hear the news. I tried to research options for you, but I came up with nothing. Isn't there some type of treatment, even if you had to go out of the country to get it?" she asked with concern.

"Unfortunately, no," I said with a sigh. "I did the same research. I realized that had I gone to the doctor earlier at the first signs of all this, I may have been able to get into an experimental treatment program. But I'm stubborn and didn't. So here I am. How's your daughter doing?" I said, changing the subject.

"Lilly's finishing up her master's degree in biology," Lisa beamed. Lilly was named after Lisa and Billy. It was a fun thing to hear how they had searched and searched for baby names, pouring over book after book.

Finally, Lisa started just writing names down to see how they looked. She meshed her and Billy's names together and came up with Lilly. It was revolutionary at the time, but now it seems common practice. At least they came up with a normal name. Some of the names kids had these days were too unique for my taste.

I always felt sorry for the kid with "Chrisley" as their name because dad was named Chris and mom was named Kelly.

Never going to find a keychain with that name!

"Wow! That's awesome. You guys must be so proud of her," I exclaimed. "She was always so smart for her age even when she was little. Remember that time we all went to Aruba for vacation? Lilly would sit for hours at the beach collecting shells that washed up. She'd put them all in size order and then proceed to tell us the name of the creature they came from. She always amazed me," I said.

"I know. Most of the time she was smarter than both of us put together and would get away with more than a kid should simply because she knew how to get out of a punishment," Billy said with a touch of pride in his voice. There was no doubt in anyone's mind that Lilly had her dad wrapped around her little finger, and Billy wouldn't have it any other way.

"Is there anything we can do for you, Edna?" Lisa asked.

What is this? A broken record?

"Actually, there is something you two can do after I'm gone. Take care of Russell. I don't mean to hound him to death to make sure he's eating or anything. Just call him up now and then. Billy, make him go play golf or catch the ballgame once a season or something," I implored.

"You got it, Edna," Billy interjected. "I've been meaning to call him up to see if he wants to hit the golf course anyway. Days, like we've been having, have been perfect for a round of golf. I'll make sure I don't let him become a hermit," he promised.

"Thanks, guys. I truly appreciate it. I feel like I'm obligating people to do things for me after I'm gone like some deathbed final request that they commit themselves begrudgingly to."

"No, no, Edna. Don't think like that. It's good of you to remind us of things we need to do while we can still do things for each other," Lisa said, trying to sound worldly.

"Hey, we'd better get going and let you get some rest. Your cute nurse, Jonathan, said that we needed to start wrapping things up. We're sorry if we kept you longer than you wanted," Lisa said.

"Oh, he is a cute one, but such a pain in the ass worrier. Thanks for coming. It was good to see you."

Who sounds like a broken record now?

Tom was the next person to come over to chat. It was like a parade at the coffin. Each person kept an eye out to see how long the line was knowing they needed to make the obligatory visit to the dead. This time though, the dead was still alive.

"Hi, Edna." He said occupying the chair Lisa had just vacated. "You're probably sick of hearing this, but how are you doing? Is there anything I can do for you to help?" he asked.

"Oh, Tom. You're right. Every single person tonight has asked me how they can help. What can they do? Is there something I need? Frankly, I'm just tired. I've asked Billy and Lisa to make sure Russell doesn't wither away. I've asked Jake to keep an eye on Delores." I watched Tom's face turn red, and I knew he was thinking of the debacle of a relationship he tried to have with Delores.

Way to go, Edna.

"Uh, I mean..." I stammered.

"It's okay, Edna. I totally get it. Jake is a much better match for Delores if you ask me. I'm comfortable being single. Don't get me wrong, Delores is a great lady. It's just she's too outgoing for me. My days are spent fixing things around the house, watching historical documentaries, and reading for the most part. Too many people kind of bind me up inside. I need my quiet time," He stated matter-of-factly.

"Speaking of fixing things around the house, Tom," I said, covering up my embarrassment at the mention of Delores. "I was wondering if you could look around my house to see if there is anything that needs repair. The kids and I have decided to sell the house, and I want to make sure there won't be any issues with an inspection. It's almost paid off so they'll be able to get a nice chunk of change from the sale. They've decided to put the money away in case mom needs help down the road. I still can't believe she's driving at her age." I stopped myself from saying that I couldn't believe she was still around, and that I'm the one dying.

"Sure thing, Edna," Tom said earnestly. "I'll be happy to do that. I know you've always taken good care of the place, so there shouldn't be too much to do. Do you want me to call any of my contacts to help with moving out any furniture or to do a whole-house cleaning? You know, to make the place really shine for any buyers." Tom was so down to earth but not very tactful. He did not see any sense in beating around the bush in matters such as this. It was refreshing. Kevin and Amelia were too emotional to think practically when it came to the house and its belongings.

"That would be wonderful, Tom," I told him, impressed by his straightforwardness. "Can you also give Kevin and Amelia the name of any auction company that takes care of the contents of a house once they've gone through what they want to keep?"

"Yep, I can do that too. I know the perfect place. I'll make sure to give them their business card the next time I see them." As soon as the words came out of his mouth, Tom looked horrified. He realized that the next time he would see Kevin or Amelia would be at my funeral. Tom may be keen on keeping facts, but he did have a heart and tried very hard not to hurt people's feelings.

"I'm so sorry, Edna. What I meant was…"

"Stop, Tom. It's all right. I know exactly what you meant, and it's what I needed you to say," I said in a comforting tone. I get that this whole thing is not pleasant for people. This *party* is definitely out of the norm, but you and I live in the real world, and real things still need to get done even as we leave."

"Thanks, Edna. It's just I've never been around anyone facing what you're facing. My grandparents died before I could ever remember them. My parents only had me and once I was 18, they booted me out of the house. I haven't heard from them since. I don't know if they're alive or dead, but I figure they don't know if I am either, so we're even. I don't know what to say in these situations."

"Just say goodbye, Tom. It's why I had this party. To say goodbye and allow others to do the same, so I could see them and hear them while I was still around," I said soothingly.

"Goodbye, Edna. I'm going to miss you." It was all Tom could say as he slowly got up and made his way over to the other guests. I saw Paula walking towards me as Tom stopped by my mother to have a chat.

I must have dozed off and on as I recalled the conversation of the night before. I could hear Caroline humming softly in the living room. I knew it was late in the evening without looking to see what time it was. Time didn't seem to matter anymore. The days, hours, and seconds were winding their way to zero for me.

As I drifted off again, I wondered why my mother didn't come to talk with me at the party.

DAY TWENTY-FOUR

Judy came in to administer more morphine. I woke up as she was grabbling the IV line to plunge more pain-numbing pharmaceuticals into my system. The gremlins started to scramble away from their feast.

"Judy?" I slurred. "Why did you become a nurse?"

Judy finished pushing the last of the medication into the tubing and looked at me. "Because I care," she said flatly.

Well, that was unexpected. Did she care? Judy? The hard-nosed, staunch nurse with the bedside manner of a prickly porcupine cared?

"I know you don't think much of me, Edna, but you and all my patients mean everything to me," she said as she pulled up the chair next to the bed. "I've been a nurse for over 15 years now. I've been a hospice nurse for over 15 years, I should say.

"I'm usually assigned four patients a year," she continued. "That's sixty patients I've administered to, taken care of, and watched die. I've bathed them, fed them, and tried to make their pain go away. I felt for their families and friends as they watched them wither away to nothing. I've watched each of them take their last breath. Some went peacefully while others struggled so much that I wanted to end their suffering by overdosing them with morphine. I never did mind you, but I always thought how much easier it would have been on them if I had. I watched them cry, curse, and scream at God about the unfairness of the illness that was taking their lives.

"I've seen the toll death takes on their once happy family. I've watched helpless husbands wring their hands as they watch their wives slip away into nothingness. I've watched wives beg God not to take their husbands away. I've watched young couples at a loss as to why their child got cancer at such a young age and was taken from them.

"I've watched you too, Edna. I've watched how you try to be strong for everyone even as cancer takes away pieces of you daily. I've watched how you try to get everything in neat order, so no one has to worry when you're gone. As if they'd be lost if you didn't provide a detailed roadmap of what to expect and how to handle things without you there guiding each and every step.

"All of that has taken its toll on me. I can't get attached to my patients. I need to care for them in an orderly, stale fashion just so I can survive it. Death is an ugly thing." She paused for a moment.

How is this caring? She sounds like a robot. No feeling. No understanding. No emotion.

"My first patient," she continued, "was a little boy named Ethan. He had leukemia, and he was only seven years old. The doctors tried every treatment there was. Ethan had six blood transfusions in his short life. They didn't help. His parents realized that the treatment for his tiny little body was worse than the cancer. The doctors knew it wasn't working, told the parents, and moved on to the next patient. I was called in to help with the transition. I like to call it that. I don't know why," she mused.

"Ethan had a bright smile for me every time I came into his room. I bought him a teddy bear one day hoping to cheer him up. By the time I got to him, he had taken a turn for the worse. The teddy bear wasn't going to help this time. I sat with him alongside his mother and watched him die. Silent tears streamed down my face. His mother let out a blood-curdling scream as she watched him take his last breath. I watch this child die in front of me. No number of textbooks on the subject prepared me for this. I was attached to this boy as if he were my own. My ego had gotten the better of me thinking I would be the one to save him.

"After Ethan died, I built a wall around my feelings. I realized I still could be a nurse. I could still help people. I just couldn't save them. So, Edna, whether you think so or not, I do care about you. I do want to make sure you aren't suffering. That's my purpose here. That's why I became a nurse; so that no one suffers." She ended her speech and left the room.

That was not what I was expecting from her! I'm telling you I've never heard someone explain what they do with less enthusiasm than she just did. I still don't like her. Even if she's not making me suffer.

As the morphine continued to relax my body, I wondered if Judy had ever been loved by somebody. The way she went on and on about her emotional wall made me think she hadn't.

That was sad to me. *I don't like her. Stop. Put yourself in her shoes. Could you watch helplessly as sixty people died on your watch? Fine. Don't die on her watch and make it sixty-one.*

DAY TWENTY-FIVE

The morphine that Judy gave me must have knocked me out for a long time. It was afternoon. I could tell because the sun was shining on the curtains covering my window. I could feel the heat of its rays.

So much for those out-of-norm cool days we had, that felt so nice. It's hot and muggy.

I heard a soft knock on my door as it opened. Russell stood in the doorway peering in, I assumed, to see if I were awake. "Hey, sleepyhead," he said, coming into the room.

"I stopped by yesterday evening, but Jonathan said you were still sleeping. Am I interrupting?" he asked.

"Yeah, the flowerpots need to go outside," I said with a cottonmouth.

Russell looked at me with a puzzled frown. "Huh?" he asked.

"Oh, sorry, apparently morphine plays tricks on your mind. What I meant to say was no, you're not interrupting me." My mind was still fuzzy, and I wasn't sure if what I just said made any more sense than what I had said before.

"I just wanted to stop by and apologize for not saying much to you at the party," he said. "I hadn't seen Jake and them for a while, and I was catching up. After Jonathan came around and told people that he thought it was time for us to be going, I saw everyone come over to talk to you. I figured you'd be too tired to talk with me."

"It's okay. They were there for me anyway, and you can stop by any time you'd like," I said, still trying to make my words come out properly.

"Edna, what am I going to do without you?" he said burying his face in his hands. I saw his shoulders shrugging, and I knew he was crying. He sobbed for a few minutes before he took in a deep breath and looked up at me. His eyes were bloodshot. "I'm sorry."

"I don't know why we ever split. I've been thinking about us for the past few weeks wondering why our marriage didn't work." I lay there and let him talk. I was too weak to speak anyway.

"I know we married when we were young. We were probably too young to think about the *'forever'* part of our vows. We got along fine, right? The kids brought some tension, but all married couples go through those years and turn out fine. Why didn't we? It's my fault. I should have stayed. I should have made you stay. I guess I thought if I acted like the man of the house, you'd fall into the typical woman's role. I should have known better. The reason I fell in love with you was because you weren't like that. You were always so strong. You always gave me a piece of your mind whenever you thought I fell out of line. Why did I want to change you?" Russell rambled on.

"I don't think I can handle this, Edna. How am I going to be able to handle Kevin and Amelia? I don't want to be a single grandparent to Henry and Gracie. I don't want you to die. I still love you, Edna. I've been such an ass. Please, Edna, don't leave me," he broke down once again.

"Stop being so fucking selfish, Russell," I blurted out. "I'm tired. I'm dying. I can't fix everything for you like I did before. You have to step up to the plate now. You need to take charge. You have to be the one the kids call when they need advice. Stop trying to lay it back on me. I'm not going to be here!" I shouted.

I laid back on my pillow, trying to catch my breath.

This is why I divorced you. You expected too much of me. You weren't a 100 percent partner; you thought it was supposed to be 50/50. That's not how it works, buddy.

As my breath slowly returned to its jagged-normal self, I turned to face Russell again. "Don't expect me to apologize for my outburst, Russell. Everyone needs to realize that I'm not going to be around much longer. Everyone has to stop trying to take from me what I can no longer give. I'm not the glue anymore. Someone else needs to fill that role, and when that glue comes to the kids, it has to be you."

"You're right, Edna," Russell sounded deflated. "I'm sorry for my selfishness. I just... I don't know what to say. I wasn't there when my mother died. You know that. I just got the phone call from Dad, hopped on the plane, and went to her funeral. Dad seemed to know what to do, and I never asked him for any details. I guess I should have," Russell laid his head on the bed next to me.

I reached over and started stroking his hair. My anger subsided. I couldn't stay mad at him forever.

Ha! You don't have forever.

The repeated action of my stroking his hair lulled me to sleep again. I felt Russell bend over and kiss my cheek before I faintly heard the door close.

DAY TWENTY-SIX

Mom came by to check on me. She used the excuse that she had left her sweater during the party. Mom always had a sweater on if the temperature reached anything below eighty degrees. She also complained it was too hot if the temperature reached anything above eighty-five degrees.

"Edna, I want to talk to you about something," she said. Here it was. The real reason she stopped by.

"Yes, Mother," I said in a tone that I truly didn't want to hear what she was about to say.

"Have you decided whether Pastor Randy is going to speak at your funeral?"

Ah, and here it is. She just couldn't let you have planned something all by yourself without her input. Stop it. It's your mother. Of course, she wants input.

"Um, not really, Mom. I figured Mr. Thorn from the funeral home was going to take care of all that."

"Well, he's not. I called over there the other day to ask him what the program was going to be, and he made no mention whatsoever about delivering any kind of scripture."

Of course, you called the funeral home.

"I think it's preposterous that he put very little scripture in the program," she said fiercely.

"Calm down, Mom," I said trying to deflate her anger. "You can call Mr. Thorn back and tell him I said that it was okay if you picked out some additional scripture to be read by Pastor Randy, if he'd like to preside over the funeral, that is." That seemed to have a positive effect on her. She sat down in the chair and let out a little huff.

I didn't care for Pastor Randy too much. I didn't care for the whole God thing at that moment. God was making me die. God was the one who had all the power, yet he just let humanity suffer. What kind of God does that? I thought he was supposed to be a loving, caring God. What happened? Why was he taking me away from my family? Didn't he know I needed to be here to watch my grandkids grow up? Didn't he know that I wasn't supposed to die before my mother? That's the circle of life, right? It wasn't fair, and I was getting angry about it. I didn't want to leave yet, dammit.

"Thank you, Edna. I already spoke to Pastor Randy, and he said he'd be happy to officiate your funeral."

Of course, you did.

"He was a tad upset that you hadn't been to church in months, and I'm sure he expects a donation, but I'll take care of that." She said, happy with herself for getting the last bit of control in.

She sat there in her smugness for a minute or two before she focused on me again. Her expression softened, and her eyes welled up with tears.

"My baby girl," she choked. "What am I going to do without you?"

"You're going to live, Mom. You're going to live a long time," I continued, catching my breaths between sentences. "You're going to see Gracie and Henry grow up. You're going to tell them about me, especially Henry. He's not going to remember me. Gracie will lose a lot of her memories of me. You must keep those memories for them. You're going to be the one that Kevin and Amelia turn to when they wonder, *'what Mom would say?'*."

"That's not what I meant, Edna," she stated. "Do you have any idea what it's like for me right now?"

Why was everyone worrying about what they were going through? I'm the one being eaten alive by cancer!

"I'm your mother," she continued. "I carried you for nine months. I made sure that I didn't eat or drink or do anything that I thought would harm you as I carried you. Once you were born, your father and I doted on you. We thought we would have other children, but God didn't see it that way."

"We made sure you had everything. We made sure you went to the best schools. We made sure we saw all your plays and recitals, even the ones where you weren't very good at, like ballet. You were a terrible ballerina, Edna." She chuckled at the memory.

I only slightly remember being in ballet class. I just wanted to be able to stand on my toes, but it never worked out. I didn't like the tutus or light pink leotards. I didn't like spinning around in circles; that always made me dizzy.

"I worried about everything in your life." She resumed her speech. "I worried about your career path. I worried about your marriage to Russell. I worried about the boyfriends before him while you were in high school, praying fervently that you wouldn't get pregnant."

Gee, thanks mom for the trust factor.

"I worried when you were pregnant with Kevin and Amelia. I even worried when you had that knee surgery after you and Russell got divorced. If you remember, you couldn't get around for a few days, and I was the one that came over to take care of you."

I remember, Mom. The knee surgery was supposed to be an outpatient procedure. The doctor was just going in to clean up some tissue that was building around my kneecap. Turns out, while he was cleaning, his blade slipped, and he nicked a tendon. He didn't cut through it or anything, just cut it enough that I had to be immobile for a few days afterward.

"Stupid doctor." She proceeded with her memory lane trip. "All I'm trying to say, Edna, is that it's hard for a mother to see her child like you are. I'm ninety-two years old. I've lived a long time. I am the one who is supposed to be lying where you are now. You are supposed to be on the other side of that bed, sitting in this chair. That's the order of things." She stopped abruptly and sucked in her breath.

"Yes, Mom. This sucks." I tried to explain. "I wasn't prepared for this either. And I surely wasn't prepared to hear that I had such a short time left. As I told others, I know I should have gone to the doctor sooner. I know I should have listened to my body, but I didn't, and this is where we are." I had to stop to catch my breath.

I tried to calm myself down. I knew I shouldn't be getting angry at my mom. I knew I shouldn't have gotten angry at Russell.

Maybe it was the side effects of the morphine. Maybe it was the gremlins eating away the nice side of me and leaving all the nastiness. Maybe, I was just tired of people trying to tell me how hard it was on them. How are they going to deal with life? What this is doing to them.

I am the one dying. Am I being the selfish one here? Am I so caught up in myself that I just wanted a little sympathy and maybe some comfort?

"Mom, can you just put your feelings aside for a few days? Can you just be here with me?" I asked solemnly. "You're strong, Mom. You can do this. You have to do this. I get my resolve from you, you know?"

"Resolve?" she quipped back at me. "Try stubbornness." She chuckled.

"That too, Mom. That too." I closed my eyes for a moment or two. Or so I thought. The morphine and the emotional conversation with my mother had taken their toll on me, and I fell fast asleep.

DAY TWENTY-SEVEN

Kevin and Amelia came by the next day. I heard Judy tell them not to stay too long.

They can stay as long as they want, Judy! They're my kids.

"Hey, Mom," Kevin said as he and Amelia walked into the room. The look on their faces told me they weren't prepared for what they saw. I was getting thin quickly. Thinner than I was a few days ago, and they noticed right away.

"Mom!" Amelia sounded frantic. "Why are you so thin?"

"I can't eat much, honey." I tried to sound normal. If normal was even a thing now for me. "Don't worry, I'm not hungry. The morphine suppresses my appetite a lot."

Amelia came over and hugged me. By the feel of her hug, I could tell she was afraid to squeeze too hard. She held on to me for a few minutes, not wanting to let go.

I didn't want her to let go either. I feebly put my arms around her and patted her back. "It's okay, honey. It's okay." I told her gently.

Amelia stood up and stepped aside so Kevin could give me a hug. He too was afraid to hug me too hard. He loosened his hug quicker than his sister had.

"We just wanted to stop by and see how you were doing," Kevin said, starting the conversation. "Dad called yesterday and told me that maybe we should stop by." I know he was stopping short of saying *before it's too late*, and I could tell those words almost came out.

"It's okay, Kevin. I'm nearing the end. I'm glad you both are here." I tried not to sound too dramatic, but I know neither one of my children was prepared for this. As their mother, I tried to shield them from this. Come to think of it, I don't think either one of them had ever attended a funeral.

When my father died, they were too young to take them to see him. Russell and I decided to leave them at home with a sitter. We didn't want them to disrupt the service. Kids that age don't understand what's going on, and they would be in their own little worlds asking too many questions of the guests.

"I wanted to let you know that I spoke with Tom at the party about the house. He's going to stop by and check everything to see if any repairs need to be done before you two put it on the market. He also is going to call you, Kevin, with some people he knows that will help auction off what you all don't want and to have a cleaning company come in and give the house a good, deep cleaning."

Amelia started to cry as I spoke about the house being put up for sale. She had agreed with Kevin that it was the best thing to do. Neither one of them could see a reason to keep it because they each had their own place. I know it was a hard decision. Did they want to keep it and be reminded of me every time they walked through the door? Or did they want to sell it and constantly think about strangers living here and doing whatever they wanted to make this house their home?

"Do we have to sell the house right away, Mom?" Amelia asked after her tears subsided.

"Not if you don't want to, honey," I said sympathetically. "If you want to wait a few months, that's fine with me. I just wouldn't wait too long. Most people don't want to buy a house around the holidays."

With that, Amelia started to cry again.

Kevin cleared his throat from the emotions that were starting to seep their way into his words. "That's a good idea, Mom. I'll talk with Tom to see what the time frame would be to get any work started that needs to be done." Kevin was always the practical one.

I dozed off and when I awoke, Kevin and Amelia were still there. Kevin had brought a chair in from the dining room so he could sit. I heard them softly talking among themselves. I couldn't quite make out the words, but certain phrases could be heard: "She's too thin." "Pastor Randy is a nice guy." "Are you getting a sitter or are you bringing Gracie?"

At the mention of my granddaughter, I woke up enough to speak. "Please don't bring the babies," I pleaded. "I don't want them to see me like this. I want them to remember our last day when we played "tucks" and with Barbie dolls. I want them to remember the laughter and the giggles, not me laying in this bed with tubing stuck all in me."

"Okay, Mom," Amelia agreed. "Henry has been asking about you though. He doesn't understand what sick is. I've tried to explain that you aren't feeling well. He wanted to make you some soup. He said I always make him soup when he's not feeling well so he thinks you'll feel better if you eat some. Chicken noodle soup, to be exact. Henry says that's the best soup."

"Just tell him I'll see him in his dreams. All he has to do is close his eyes and think of me. I'll be there," I told Amelia.

"Tell Gracie that I will also always be with her, too," I said turning towards Kevin. "She is so smart. Don't let her slack in life, Kevin. Don't be too hard on her when she makes mistakes, but don't let her wallow in them."

"I won't, Mom," he said quietly.

"Come here, you two."

Kevin and Amelia got up and came to my bedside.

"Don't be sad for me. I don't want either of you to get depressed every holiday or birthday or whatever. Don't get me wrong, I would hope you would think of me," I laughed. "But don't sit around an entire day crying. Remember me in a good way. I know I'm not a saint, and I've made mistakes in my life. Hell, I know I made mistakes raising you two. I did what I thought was best. I hope you have enjoyed having me as your mother as much as I have loved having both of you as my kids." I was the one getting too emotional now. I put my arms out, and they both hugged me at once. It was a tearful moment, to say the least.

"Okay. Enough of that," I said, clearing my throat. "You two get on home now and take care of your family. I'm going to get some rest now, and there's no sense in just sitting there watching me sleep."

"Okay, Mom," Kevin and Amelia said. "We'll see you later." With that, they both left the room.

Boy, that was tough.

You did the best you could with them. Now, it's time for them to stand for themselves. You're sleepy. I know that. Just sleep then.

DAY TWENTY-EIGHT

It was the middle of the night again.

Why can't you wake up on Jonathan's shift? He's such a great cook and is really cute. Will you stop? I don't think Jonathan wants to have a roll in the hay with you. Why not? He could jump my bones... when I'm bones. You're sick. No kidding.

I heard Caroline humming. It was strange though. It was as if she was in my room humming. I turned my head towards the sound and saw my mother sitting in the chair next to me. She just sitting in the dark, humming.

"Mom?" I questioned groggily. "What are you doing?"

"Shhh, honey," she whispered. "Go back to sleep."

I listened to her softly hum, trying to pick out the tune. It sounded like an old gospel hymn that I couldn't put my finger on. My mother never was a great singer, so I don't know why I thought she'd hum any better. The notes would rise and fall. Sometimes she'd stretch them out as if filling in the blanks because she didn't know the words.

I was comforted by her presence. I inhaled the slight, lingering scent of her perfume. The smell took me back to Christmas. I had given her the perfume then. It was Gucci. Mom scoffed at the extravagant bottle, scolding me for spending too much money. Mom always bought herself the least expensive of anything but never was stingy for anyone else. It was a trait I inherited as well. She would admonish me for never buying nice things for myself.

"You never treat yourself, Edna," she would say. "Go get a massage" or "Why don't you buy yourself a pretty dress?" I never liked dresses and mom knew it, but she was old-fashioned when it came to one's appearance.

After she had opened the bottle and smelled the perfume, she sprayed herself with it. A little spritz on her wrists and one more on the base of her neck was all she needed. She smiled when the scent hit her nostrils. "Oh, that's nice!" She had exclaimed.

The scene continued in my head. The kids were there along with my grandchildren. All my love was under one roof. I had been so content watching everyone exchange their gifts. The 'ohs' and 'ahs' could be heard between the giggles and laughter. It was a happy time. A time before I knew about the cancer. A time before the extensive coughing. A time before the gremlins. A time of sheer ignorance.

Mom's humming continued. I concentrated on each note, trying to figure out the song. I wanted to ask mom what she was humming, but the words wouldn't come out. As an avid music fan, this was pure torture.

What is that song? I don't know. Ask Mom. I can't. You do it. Well, if I can't then you can't either.

"Amazing Grace, how sweet the sound." My mom sang the words out loud.

Finally!

Mom continued the lyrics, and my mind sang along. I felt a tear fall from the corner of my eye. That was my favorite hymn. The first time I heard it, I was twenty-three years old. I had gone to church out of the blue. Something had called me into the building. I could say it was God, but at that time I had my doubts about his existence.

The choir, each one garbed in navy-blue robes with a solid white stripe on each side of the zipper, stood up and started singing the hymn. The first line caught my attention. As the choir continued each verse, the words sunk into my heart. I had been going through a rough time with Russell. I didn't want to talk to my mom about it, and my friends could offer no insight. I had been thinking of leaving him. He wanted to start a family, and I didn't. We had had a fight the night before, and we both said some nasty things to one another. I felt like I didn't have it all together; that the plans I had laid out for myself at the tender age of ten when all girls have it all figured out, were falling apart. This wasn't how I pictured my life. I was a wretch. I was a mess. How could anyone love me?

"He will my shield and portion be, as long as life endures." Those were the words that broke me and built me up at the same time. From that moment on, I knew I could continue with my marriage and be able to stand on my own two feet. Everything was going to be okay.

Mom finished humming. It was quiet for a few minutes and then I heard her get up from the chair. She put her hand on my face and cupped my cheek. "I love you, sweetie." I heard her say. I felt her lips on my forehead and her soft breath as she let out a jagged sigh.

DAY TWENTY-NINE

My days and nights started to get mixed up. I couldn't tell which nurse was coming in to change me. Yes, I needed changing. How embarrassing it was to have someone else wipe your butt and clean you. I wasn't eating by now. At least, I don't remember eating. I don't remember feeding myself. I don't remember anyone else doing it for me either.

I vaguely remember someone sticking another tube in my nose and down my throat. I could hardly swallow without gagging. It felt as if I had constant phlegm stuck in my throat. Like an oyster stuck in mid-slurp. I kept trying to hack it up. It didn't work.

Caroline had started sitting with me in my room now. The light didn't bother me for some reason. She moved the chair over to the corner of my room and would turn the lamp on beside her. She'd pick up the blanket she was crocheting for her grandson and start working on it. I could hear her humming. *Or was it my mom?* They sounded similar when either one was humming.

Caroline would put aside her project now and then and come check on me. I could feel her move my body as she checked to see if

I had soiled my sheets. She changed the pads if she needed to. She would talk to herself about me.

She'd say, "Oh, Miss Edna. Let's get this mess cleaned up now." Or if I was clean and dry, I'd hear her say, "Nothing here."

I could feel her hands check my forehead to see if I had a temperature. She'd verify her results by taking my temperature. She didn't check with a mouth thermometer either. If I cared, I had no way to show it.

I was mostly a vegetable now. Totally helpless.

This sucks! Ya think? I wish I had been hit by a bus. It would have been easier. For whom? For me, that's who! I don't want someone wiping my ass. I don't want to lay here and have all my bodily functions doing whatever they want.

Where's my control? Where's my dignity?

These nurses aren't family. They shouldn't be taking care of me. Where are my kids? I wiped their asses plenty of times. They owe me. Sure, they do. Did they ask to be born? No. You decided to bring them into this world. You are responsible for them. Just as they are responsible for the two additions to the population they produced.

"Peaches," I blurted out. "Mom, I want peaches."

What is that all about? I don't know. A peach popped into my head. A big fuzzy peach. It was a ripe one too. It dripped its juices all over me when I bit into it.

Caroline spoke to me assuredly. "I'll get you some peaches, Miss Edna. Don't you worry none."

Caroline is good people.

Yes. Yes, she is.

Go to sleep. NO! I want to wake up.

This is horrible.

Why can't I move?

DAY THIRTY

I couldn't wake up anymore. I wasn't dead yet, but I wasn't alive either. I was in the "in-between," as they called it.

Who are they? I don't know.... they.

I went through periods of complete blackness like when someone turns out the lights and your eyes haven't adjusted to the darkness. The period before your pupils absorbs the smallest traces of light so that you can make your way around in the void.

There was a coldness in the obscurity. I couldn't get warm. I started shivering. Someone must have put a blanket on me because I stopped shivering. A warming sensation came over me and the darkness started getting brighter. I saw a shadow in the light getting closer. I could make out a figure, but it was still too far away.

As it drew closer, I could recognize the features of a man. At once, I realized it was my father. "Daddy!" I exclaimed running hurriedly into his arms.

Kyle Slater, my father, had been a formidable man who died in his prime. He had joined the Marine Corps right out of high school.

He decided in his senior year to become a Marine, and that's exactly what he did. Once he made his mind up, nothing was going to stop him.

He served in the Korean War. He had been a Marine for only two years when the conflict started. In the three years that the war raged on, my father worked his way through the ranks and became a Sergeant. When the war ended, my father served one more year before leaving the Corps. Vietnam was becoming a hot issue, and he had seen his share of death and destruction.

After leaving the Corps, my father settled down into civilian life with some difficulty. He had been used to the order and discipline of military life and civilian life was too disorganized for him. He found a job working at the docks along the Gulf coast. Dock work was hard and dirty, and my father excelled in the environment.

He shared a small apartment with another Marine buddy of his until he was able to save enough money to buy a house of his own. When he applied for the loan on the house, he met my mother at the bank that was going to handle the transaction.

Banking runs in the family.

My mother and father dated for a year before my father proposed to her. My mom continued to work at the bank until I was born, and my father decided that she should stay home with me while he went to work. They used the money she made from her job at the bank to put a down payment on the house in Killian. As discussed, mom stayed home with me until I started school. Afterward, she started back at the bank until she decided to retire.

Dad made sure that he was home every night. Only occasionally would he be called into work for an emergency. He had made it clear to the company that he wanted to spend as much time as possible with his family, especially his daughter. I was his little girl, and every night when he came through the door, he'd scoop me up in his arms and swing me around.

My dad was exceedingly tall. Standing at 6'6," he made his presence known. However, he was a gentle giant when it came to me. Never once in my life did I feel like my father wanted a son, as I was their only child. I was most assuredly a daddy's girl. He wasn't ashamed that I had him wrapped around his finger.

He would sit with me for pretend teatime and read me bedtime stories. No matter how many times he read me the same story, if I asked for it, he'd read it again always with the same enthusiasm as he read it the first time. It didn't matter what we did so long as we did it together.

Dad continued to work at the docks until oil rigs started popping up in the Gulf of Mexico. He was offered a job as a foreman on one of the first rigs installed in the early 1970s. When my dad turned 60, Mom felt it was time for him to retire. He had put his time in, and it was time he started enjoying life more than just on the weekends. He made good money, and he still would have his military pension coming to him whenever he decided to start collecting it. Dad didn't want to leave. He felt his job gave him a sense of purpose and pride in the world.

I remember a hurricane coming into the Gulf, and Dad got called in to help secure the rig. The storm was fierce and was dumping a lot of rain making the rig slippery and difficult to maneuver. A piece of the rig broke loose and caught my dad in the stomach. The force of the blow knocked him to the rig floor. As he tried to get up, another piece came crashing down, hitting him in the head. He laid unconscious on that deck until another crew member found him once the storm had subsided some. The crew member was too late. My father died three days later from the injuries he sustained.

My dad put me down and smiled at me. He started to turn and walk away and then suddenly stopped. As he turned back to face me, he smiled his warm, loving smile. I never felt so much peace. He reached out his hand to me and I took it.

Epilogue- My Eulogy

Louisiana Times Obituary. Edna (nee Slater) Berman, a devoted mother and daughter, died peacefully in her sleep on July 30, 2021, at the age of 58 after a brief battle with cancer. She was surrounded by her family. Ms. Berman is proceeded in death by her father, Kyle Slater. She is survived by her mother, Pamela Slater, her son Kevin Berman and his wife Paula, and her daughter, Amelia Berman-Torez. She also leaves behind two grandchildren, Gracie Berman and Henry Berman-Torez. Ms. Berman was also surrounded by her best friend, Delores Simon, who was able to make her last days fun and enjoyable.

Ms. Berman was raised in Killian, Louisiana. She attended Killian High School and graduated in 1981. She attended Killian County College. Ms. Berman worked at First Trust Bank in Killian for 10 years before retiring early. Ms. Berman loved to spend time with her family and friends and was an avid gardener. She was known by her friends as an outgoing person who loved a variety of music and enjoyed playing trivia.

The family asks that, in lieu of flowers, donations be sent to the Killian County Red Cross. Ms. Berman sponsored this charity and wanted to see its work continued.

Family and friends wishing to pay their respects may do so at Ford's Funeral Home located at 1648 Pond Lake Dr., Killian, LA 70462. Visiting hours for viewing will be 3:00 PM-5:00 PM and 6:00 PM-8:00 PM on August 1, 2021. A funeral service will be held on August 2, 2021, at 11:00 AM with interment to immediately follow. Interment will be for family only.

www.ingramcontent.com/pod-product-compliance
Lightning Source LLC
Chambersburg PA
CBHW070509300726
48975CB00007B/2386